ONE ACTS OF NOTE 2008

ONE
ACTS
OF
NOTE 2008

An anthology of notable American
One-Act Plays

Edited by
JAMES DAMONE

CONTENTS

THE LIMP by *John Lane,* pg. 1

MOM AND DAD MEET IN HEAVEN by *John Ireland,* pg. 21

LOOK UP by *Sharon Yablon,* pg. 49

GEORGIE GETS A FACELIFT by *Dan Guyton,* pg. 59

AMERICAN INTERLUDE by *Scott Brooks,* pg. 71

RAFT OF MEDUSA-POST MODERN by *Christine Emmert,* pg. 87

SHE IS AND SHE ISN'T by *George Freek,* pg. 95

AMARILLO ROSE by *David Miguel Estrada,* pg. 113

THE HOMELESS SECRETARY by *Gerry Sheridan,* pg. 135

DAWNLESS DAYS by *Olivia Arieti,* pg. 151

A GOOD KID by *Bill Mesce Jr,* pg. 165

LAST DANCE by *Carol Schlanger,* pg. 193

THE SELLING OF THE SOUL by *Walter Dalton,* pg. 205

JETTISON by *Brendan Andolsek Bradley,* pg. 213

4 DAYS IN BED by *Jonson Kuhn & Ariel Marks,* pg. 225

THE LIMP

John Lane

THE LIMP was first produced at Stages Theatre (Fullerton, CA) and Cedar Lane Theatre (Bethesda, MD) in 2007.

CAST OF CHARACTERS

ROGER: *Male, 20s, an insecure junior executive.*

CLAUDINE: *Female, 20s, an aggressive junior executive.*

HOWARD: *Male, 50s, a no-nonsense, top executive type.*

At Rise CLAUDINE is seated alone at a table in an upscale restaurant sipping a drink. ROGER enters and hurriedly walks to the table. He walks with a faint limp.

ROGER: Sorry, Claudine. I'm late, aren't I?

CLAUDINE: Yes, you are. Didn't we say noon?

He hands her a folder.

ROGER: I suppose I could have faxed these papers to you, but since you're just a few blocks across town, I thought –

CLAUDINE, *Overlaps:* Anyway, we both have to eat lunch. *Pause.* By the way, Roger, did you hurt you leg?

ROGER: My leg? No, not at all.

CLAUDINE: I thought I saw you limp a bit – when you walked in here just now.

ROGER: A limp – I've always had that limp.

CLAUDINE: You have? I guess I've never noticed.

ROGER: I'm sure you noticed. You just chose not to say anything.

CLAUDINE: What happened? Sprain your ankle?

ROGER: A childhood thing. A birth defect. One leg is shorter than the other.

CLAUDINE: Really. I just never noticed.

ROGER: Well, you obviously noticed today.

CLAUDINE: Maybe I never saw you walk before. Come to think of it, I usually see you behind a desk. In fact, I find it difficult to think of you, except behind a desk.

ROGER: Really, Claudine, I'm quite capable of locomotion. It's just that …

CLAUDINE, *thinks:* Shorter than the other? Which leg is shorter, the right or the left?

ROGER: Really, Claudine, does it make a difference? I have a limp – let's leave it at that!

CLAUDINE: Really, Roger, I'm just curious. I just notice that when you entered …

ROGER: I looked like a gimp. Is that your point?

CLAUDINE: Your gimp – er, I mean your limp – it's hardly …

ROGER, *overlaps testily:* It's the right one. The right leg is shorter.

CLAUDINE: As you said, it really doesn't matter. It's really barely noticeable – except of course, when you walk.

ROGER, *gathers his thoughts:* You know, when I was a kid, I hardly knew I had a limp. I never thought I was different. And then one day I realized.

CLAUDINE: What happened?

ROGER: I went to a Catholic school. On Halloween, we would play this game. We would all be dressed up in our costumes and go into the gym. And Sister Immaculata would come in, and have us all march around in a circle.

CLAUDINE: A circle? Why?

ROGER: She would try to guess who we were? When she guessed one of us, that kid had to leave the circle. Finally, the last one left marching got a prize. *Pause.* I was in second grade when we did this. I had this really great lion's costume. I spent a lot of time getting ready – the mask, the mane, the whiskers – all that. I put my heart into it. But then this Mark, who I thought was my friend, said to me – no matter how great your costume is, Sister's going to guess you first.

CLAUDINE: Children can be cruel.

ROGER: He said as soon as you take two steps, she'll know it's you. *Pause.* Up to that point, I never realized that everyone noticed the way I walked. They had all been lying to me. My parents too – lying.

CLAUDINE: About your limp? How can you say "lying"? They wanted to spare your feelings.

ROGER: I never trusted people after that. They won't tell you what they're really thinking.

CLAUDINE: That's ridiculous. We don't have to confront people about their defects. Do you go up to an ugly woman and tell her she's ugly?

ROGER: Of course not. I wouldn't go up to a stranger.

CLAUDINE: I'm not a stranger. Would you tell me I'm ugly?

ROGER: You're obviously not ugly, Claudine.

CLAUDINE: But if I were, and if you were a close friend, would you?

ROGER: I might suggest something – something remedial – like "Why don't you try a new hairstyle, Claudine?" Something like that.

CLAUDINE: The point is – you're overreacting. *Thinks.* You were speaking hypothetically? About my hair?

ROGER: Hypothetically? Of course. I just gave you an example – out of the blue. *Looks at her hair.* You hair is quite – okay, I suppose.

CLAUDINE: "Okay," you suppose?! Jesus, Roger, you really know how to flatter a girl.

ROGER: If I said your hair was wonderful, you probably wouldn't believe me.

CLAUDINE: Obviously, that event with the nun left its mark on you: this thing about not trusting people.

ROGER: You know how it is in the corporate world these days. You trust someone, a colleague whom you thought you knew – but now, you don't dare turn your back on him. You might end up with a knife between your shoulder blades.

CLAUDINE: Are you referring to the Murchison account?

ROGER, *warily:* The Murchison account? I suppose that could be part of it.

CLAUDINE: The Murchison account seemed to have slipped through the cracks until recently. Now it's on everyone's mind. We eventually had to deal with it.

ROGER, *confidential tone:* Well conversation is more secure here. In my office nowadays, one never knows. The economy, the threat of downsizing, those merger rumors… It's become downright Darwinian over there.

CLAUDINE: It's affected our firm as well. There've been rumblings.

ROGER: You've heard – rumblings?

CLAUDINE: About the merger? Well some rumblings, but nothing concrete. And also rumors. Of course, there's always rumors.

ROGER: Hmm. Rumblings are sometimes more accurate than rumors. And you're in a better position than I am to know what's going on. At our place, it's unbridled paranoia. I walk into Norman's office the other day, he immediately covers up something on his desk. For God's sake, does he think I'm going to pull out my microfilm camera and photograph his precious documents?

CLAUDINE: These things can get out of hand. Insecure people doing petty things…

ROGER: Case in point, I always thought Brendan McCarthy and I had a good working relationship. But then I see him in the hall Tuesday with Rodriquez, talking very intently. They see me coming, and snap! Just like that, they clam up.

CLAUDINE: You think it was about …

ROGER: Murchison? It could be, of course. I'm just giving you an example of the atmosphere over there.

CLAUDINE: You realize, of course, this Murchison thing was not entirely your fault.

ROGER: I had basic responsibility, of course. But really…

CLAUDINE: Let's face it – it was a major snafu – from start to finish. And as a result, our Murchison Foundation loses twenty-two percent of its funding for this year. There's a lot of blame to go around. But of course, your name always comes up.

ROGER: Comes up? My name?

CLAUDINE: For Christ's sake, Roger, what do you expect? You were the point man. Your name is linked with Murchison.

ROGER: It was a lousy year. We all thought the market would recover.

CLAUDINE: Well it obviously didn't. You people had responsibility for financial advisement. At least, that's what they pay you for. *Pause.* And needless to say, it's had a domino effect on our firm as well.

ROGER: Perhaps "rippling effect" would be a better term, Claudine. "Domino effect" suggests a toppling of something. *Laughs nervously.* Your firm is in no danger of being "toppled."

CLAUDINE: Lighten up, Roger. It's just an expression – an analogy. I didn't know you were so picky about language.

ROGER: "Toppling" is very strong term.

CLAUDINE: My word was "domino." You brought up "toppling." *Pause.* My God, why are we arguing petty semantics when this merger is looming over your firm like an albatross?

ROGER: Albatross? Then you HAVE heard something?

CLAUDINE: Logically speaking, merger or not, there will be layoffs. And it likely will affect my company as well. It's the times we live in, Roger. It's not a time for weak-kneed wimps.

ROGER: Wimps? Are you saying I'm a wimp?

CLAUDINE: What do you mean? A wimp just because you have a limp? I implied no such thing. *Pause.* But I do appreciate your sharing that story with me today – about the nun and the costumes and – your limp.

ROGER: Well, I'd appreciate it if you would keep it in confidence.

CLAUDINE: It's quite touching. I actually never thought of you as a sensitive person.

ROGER: Well, I'm certainly not insensitive. *Thinks.* You think I'm insensitive?

CLAUDINE: I suppose you're just a very focused person, perhaps over-focused, perhaps even aloof. I would say quite self-involved, not always aware of the big picture.

ROGER: Not aware of the big picture?

CLAUDINE: There were certain market indicators that you missed. You had the Murchison account unnecessarily exposed.

ROGER: With you, it always comes down to Murchison doesn't it, Claudine?

CLAUDINE: I've obviously hit on a raw nerve. But there's no getting around it, we'll all have to deal with the fallout from this Murchison affair.

ROGER: Affair? Aren't you being a bit melodramatic? It hardly qualifies as an affair. There was no "scandal" involved. It had no secret agenda. It was an account that took a hit in a bear market. Nothing more, nothing less.

CLAUDINE : Well, I won't dwell on it – at this time, since it obviously upsets you. *Long pause.* You were Catholic? I never thought of you as – Catholic. I always thought of you as being... *She thinks.* Episcopalian – yes, Episcopalian.

ROGER: Those nuns could be cruel.

CLAUDINE: Hmm, maybe even Presbyterian. Yes, Presbyterian suits you. They're rather staunch, colorless types.

ROGER: You think I'm "colorless"?

CLAUDINE: In the investment business, staunch and colorless would be considered assets.

ROGER: Well, sorry to disappoint you, Claudine, but I am Catholic, baptized and confirmed.

CLAUDINE: I usually think of Catholics as being more – ethnic. You know, Latino or Mediterranean types…

ROGER: I was Irish on my mother's side. I guess Irish is not considered ethnic anymore.

CLAUDINE: Of course Brendan McCarthy – your buddy, or should I say, former buddy – his name is very Irish, very ethnic.

ROGER, *thinks:* McCarthy. I never thought he would be the one to screw me over.

CLAUDINE: Come on, Roger. Screw you over? Just because you saw him talking with Rodriquez in the hallway? Now YOU'RE getting paranoid. This Murchison thing is really getting to you.

HOWARD enters the restaurant and looks around for someone, but apparently does not find him.

ROGER, *sees Howard:* Christ. There's Howard Gardiner from corporate. He just walked in. What is he doing here?

CLAUDINE: He's already spotted us. He's coming over.

Howard comes to the table. Roger stands to shake hands. They ad lib greetings.

ROGER: Howard, you know Claudine here?

HOWARD: Of course. In fact, she was at a meeting with us last week. *He shakes her hand.*

ROGER: Meeting – last week?

HOWARD: Mind if I join you for a few minutes? I'm early. Meeting McCarthy here at twelve thirty…

ROGER: Of course not. Sit down. We haven't ordered yet. *Warily.* McCarthy? Something important brewing?

HOWARD, *sits down:* Not really. More of a social lunch. But McCarthy and I always end up in some heated discussion about this or that…

CLAUDINE: The merger, for example? That's the big topic these days.

HOWARD: Frankly, I'm tired of all this goddamn scuttlebutt on the merger. All these scenarios. Merger or not, I say it's time to get rid of the dead wood, the namby-pambies who can't pull their weight. *Pause.* Oh by the way, Roger, I thought I saw you limp getting out of the elevator a few days ago. Hurt your leg skiing or something?

ROGER: No, actually I've always limped a bit.

CLAUDINE: One leg is shorter than the other.

ROGER, *annoyed:* Claudine, I don't think Howard cares about…

HOWARD: The right leg or the left?

CLAUDINE, *pause:* The right one.

HOWARD: Just curious. A limp is really not much of a handicap. I imagine you can do – most things. *Chuckles – to Claudine.* But I guess if we have to run any marathons in the near future, we won't be depending on our Roger here.

ROGER: Well, I'm certainly able to…

HOWARD, *overlaps:* That goes without saying. People with limps have gone on to lead healthy, useful lives. *Pause.* I recall a young ensign – served under me back in my Navy days. Crackerjack man with a computer. Had a limp of some sort. Can't recall if it was right or left leg. But I'll tell you one thing: he never mentioned his limp and neither did we. And that in a nutshell, is what I think about limps.

ROGER: Howard, it has never affected my performance in any way. I assure you that I …

HOWARD, *overlaps:* Speaking of performance, and while I've got you two here together, there're a few things about this Murchison account I'd like to go over. We need to get things shipshape.

ROGER, *nervously:* Claudine and I were just discussing that same topic. As I was telling her, we've got to rethink our investment targets for the coming year.

HOWARD: Exactly. Set new goals for the year. Realistic goals this time. Re-deploy some of the funds into a safer harbor, so to speak.

CLAUDINE: And I think Roger's just the man to do it.

HOWARD: Just as I keep telling the Board, Roger here shouldn't be the fall guy on Murchison.

ROGER: Fall guy?

CLAUDINE: I said the same thing, there's plenty of blame to go around.

HOWARD: But Roger of course, has the lion's share of that blame. When the ship goes off course, you have to blame the navigator.

ROGER, *overlaps:* The equity market last year – who knew it would underperform like it did.

HOWARD: Well, goddamn it, there were some market indicators that did point to the downturn. As I always say, before you set sail, you look at the weather report. Municipal bonds would have been a safer harbor for some of the foundation funds. *Calms down.* But as they say, hindsight and four bucks will buy you a latte grande.

CLAUDINE: In Roger's defense, I can say that he has never denied his share of responsibility in the whole matter.

ROGER: Of course not. Mistakes were made. I can't deny that.

HOWARD: I'll tell you one thing, I like a man who can stand up and take his share of the blame. A man who is willing to go down with the ship…

ROGER: Down with the ship?

CLAUDINE: If and when the merger takes place, and when all the dust has cleared, I think Roger will be one of those still standing.

ROGER, *nervously, tries to make a joke:* Maybe standing in the unemployment line.

HOWARD, *distracted:* I was just thinking. If one of your legs IS shorter than the other, and you were to stand a long time in an unemployment line or some such thing, would you tend to put most of your weight on the good leg or the bad leg?

ROGER: Well, neither leg is really "bad." One leg is simply shorter.

CLAUDINE: But I suppose the short leg would be considered the bad one.

HOWARD: Hmm, it's an interesting philosophical question – in any case, constantly putting more weight on one leg – wouldn't that do something to the spine – over the long run? Cause permanent damage?

ROGER: I've never had any problem… spine-wise, that is.

HOWARD: Well you certainly appear to be in relatively good shape. Other than that nasty limp of yours…

ROGER: Nasty?

CLAUDINE: I think Roger can carry his weight, so to speak.

ROGER: Howard, I'd like to say, that in my eight years with the firm, the client has always come first. I hope the Murchison people realize that. In fact, when push comes to shove, I place the client ahead of the firm.

HOWARD: To me, the client and the firm are one and the same. Without clients, you have no firm; without a firm you obviously have no clients. And in your case, we can say: if Murchison sneezes, you get a cold.

CLAUDINE, *looking around:* I still don't see McCarthy. I guess he's late.

HOWARD: Punctuality is not McCarthy's strong suit. One time, waiting for him delayed the Farnsworth board meeting a full ten minutes. By Christ, you don't keep the captain waiting on the bridge. And whether he realizes it or not, today is a crucial meeting for him.

ROGER: I thought you said it was social.

HOWARD: I wanted a casual setting. We might have to let him go. This merger and all. I wanted to more or less feel him out today, assess his capabilities. We're thinking about transferring him to the Duluth office. I don't like tossing a man overboard if we have a lifeboat available.

ROGER, *with fear and loathing:* Duluth?

HOWARD: Well, the merger's certainly not a done deal by any means. But we are making preliminary lists. There's always downsizing following a merger. Obviously some people WILL be let go. If you reduce the size of the fleet, you don't need as many hands on deck. *Pause.* Needless to say, what I'm telling you now goes no further than this table. Loose lips sink ships.

CLAUDINE / ROGER: Of course.

HOWARD: Frankly speaking, Roger, this Murchison account might have saved your sorry ass. At one point there was talk about letting you go. There's no doubt the Murchison account took a hit last year. But to unravel that mess, we need someone who knows where the bodies are buried, so to speak.

ROGER: Bodies?

HOWARD: Someone who understands the whole mess. A navigator who knows where the reefs are. That's you. Your game plan last year was misguided, and you certainly should have stayed out of the tech stocks for Christ's sake. But you're the only one who understands those goddamn options and hedge funds. You know the people over at Murchison, and you made them some real money in 1999. Of course, it didn't take any talent to make money in 1999.

ROGER: I really appreciate this, Howard.

HOWARD: On top of that, Old Lady Murchison likes you for some goddamn reason. And that old bag is not the easiest person on the

Board to deal with. No, Roger, you're probably going stay on with the firm, merger or not. You're a liability, but you're OUR liability.

ROGER, *greatly relieved:* Thank you, Howard. Thank you.

HOWARD: By the way, Roger, do you play golf?

ROGER: No, I really never …

HOWARD: Golf. Great asset. Dealing with clients, board members. All that.

ROGER: I suppose I could learn. I…

HOWARD, *overlaps:* Out on the course you see what a man is made of. I consider golf a metaphor for life. Show me a man on his bad day, coming into the back nine already fifteen over par, trying to get out of a goddamn sand trap, and I can tell you how that man handles a corporate crisis.

ROGER: I'm sure I could take some lessons and…

HOWARD: Then again, with that bad back of yours…

ROGER: My back is fine, Howard.

HOWARD: I suppose with a golf cart and all, you could…

ROGER, *overlaps:* I wouldn't need a golf cart. Walking is not a problem.

HOWARD: That what I like to hear. When I see those perfectly healthy namby pambies grinding down the fairway in their precious little sun-roofed golf carts, I could puke.

ROGER: I would never use a cart.

HOWARD: That's what I like to hear, a man walking on his own two feet. But then again, with your back already weak, I wouldn't advise carrying clubs. Besides that, I always say, let the caddy make a living.

ROGER: I would certainly use a caddy, Howard.

HOWARD: Well then, that's settled. *To Claudine.* By the way, Claudine, I hope we haven't bored you here with our man talk?

CLAUDINE: Women do play golf, Howard.

HOWARD: And well they should. Great game for up-and-coming female executives like yourself. *Pause.* Do you know how many deals are made on the fairway and in the locker room? *Thinks.* I suppose the locker room could be a problem in your case. *Reminisces.* Worst thing the Navy ever did, letting women go to sea. "His and her" latrines, then pregnancies... what the hell did they expect? You have ovulating women and a vessel full of able-bodied seamen in the South Pacific for three months? That's a Petri dish for permanent personnel problems. Thank the Christ I retired when I did.

CLAUDINE: I think women can perform almost every duty that...

HOWARD, *overlaps:* Of course they can. I like women who can hold their own at the conference table. Not afraid to be heard. Take last week. I liked the way you spoke up about Murchison at that meeting.

ROGER: There was a meeting last week about Murchison?

HOWARD: Just one of the items on the agenda. Claudine here can fill you in. *Looks across the room.* Ahoy there. I just spotted McCarthy. He just came in the door.

Howard and Roger both rise.

HOWARD: Okay, you two. All this stuff is confidential. Don't forget. You got your orders: keep the ship on course. *He turns to leave, but then returns briefly.* By the way, Roger, about that limp — contact my office. We'll get you a handicapped space in the garage.

Roger and Claudine look at each other as Howard walks away.

CLAUDINE: Roger, this is your lucky day.

ROGER: Well, at least I didn't get sent to Duluth.

CLAUDINE: You lucky son of a bitch. Because you screwed up on Murchison, you're going to survive the merger. And because of that tiny limp of yours, you're getting handicapped parking.

ROGER: So what was that meeting about last week?

CLAUDINE: They brought me in at the last moment. I suppose because of my connection with the Murchison and the foundation.

ROGER: Murchison was on the agenda, and I wasn't invited?

CLAUDINE: Actually, YOU were on the agenda. Your name, that is. *Pause.* As Howard said, there was some talk of letting you go.

ROGER: I bet McCarthy led that attack.

CLAUDINE: Actually, McCarthy was one of the few people who defended you.

ROGER: Few people? Well, I hope you were on my side in that little discussion.

CLAUDINE: Really Roger, I could hardly defend you and the Murchison performance last year. But Old Lady Murchison praised you to the skies. I think she's got a thing for you.

ROGER: Thing for me? Christ, she's seventy-five, if she's a day.

CLAUDINE: Maybe it's that limp. With a limp you look vulnerable, and that can be attractive to a lot of women. Brings out their maternal instinct…

ROGER: I've been here eight years and had the limp. I'd almost forgotten about it. Why is my limp suddenly becoming such a big deal? I've always hated that limp.

CLAUDINE: I guess because it's always been a big deal – with you. *Pause.* You never did finish your story – the Halloween costumes, the nun. How did it turn out? Were you the first one she picked to leave the circle?

ROGER: No, actually she recognized my friend, Mark, first. He was the tallest kid in the class, an easy target, I guess. I was picked tenth. I guess a lion with a limp is not that unusual. I even got a prize.

CLAUDINE: A lion with a limp, and you get a prize. You were a lucky bastard even back then. And now it's got you job insurance, a handicapped parking space, and it looks like you're going to be playing golf with Howard Gardiner.

ROGER: Jesus. I hate golf.

CLAUDINE: You can't win them all, Roger. But learning golf sure as hell beats Duluth.

ROGER, *thinks:* Maybe, if I started using a cane. Guys with canes don't usually play golf, do they?

CLAUDINE: Hmm. A cane? Brilliant. You're raising your limp to a new level. Personally, I think a man with a cane looks very masculine. Crutches are wimpy, but a cane – very macho.

Throughout the following speeches, the lights gradually fade.

ROGER: Macho. I like that. Let's see, what kind of cane? A dark color, definitely dark. Dark commands respect. And maybe some carving on it. Like a shillelagh. After all, I am part Irish. *Beat.* Naw, a shillelagh's a bit too ornate. Might give the wrong message. Something simpler, more classic – like a lion's head. Yeah, that's it, a lion's head on the handle. A lion.

CLAUDINE: Yes, a lion with a limp.

BLACKOUT

MOM AND DAD MEET IN HEAVEN

John Ireland

MOM, a stunning young woman dressed in a black shirt and slacks, strides onto STAGE RIGHT and stands behind a chair. DAD, a tired and aging man, sits in a chair on STAGE LEFT.

MOM, *to the audience:* As the title of this play implies, we are cutting to the chase because that is always where life ends up. It is important that I acknowledge you... address you because you... you are what this is all about. You are what this man's life was all about. *She glances at Dad.* It is your approval that was the mirror he could never stop gazing into. It is this place, this stage, this here and now that he loved beyond all else. More than sex, more than wealth, more than children... it was to be here, to be in front of you, acting, that was his core. Why bring this all up now, sixteen years since he died... now when the memory of him is even dimmer? No importance really. Like all art, there is no value in what happens tonight... unless of course, you decide otherwise. Unless something happens here...and it pricks your skin... and a little of your own blood seeps onto the stage. *Mom looks up at the sky and feels something hot running through her veins. Dad, as if waking from sleep, looks over and sees Mom, he rises and calls to her.*

DAD, *at first unsure:* Elaine?!

Mom turns and looks at Dad.

MOM: John?!

He moves center stage but stops from crossing over to her.

DAD: Elaine... it is you... oh... geez...

Mom approaches Dad, but with less enthusiasm.

MOM: John... yes it's me. And it is you.

DAD: Yes, of course it's me. *They stop five feet from each other... look at each other... then at themselves.*

MOM: Yes... it is... us... but I'm so much younger.

DAD: Yes, I can see.

MOM: Why?

DAD: I don't know.

MOM: But we were both old when we died.

DAD: Yes.

MOM: And you died years before me.

DAD: Yes.

MOM: So why aren't we the same? Or almost the same?

DAD: I don't know. Sometimes when I run into someone from the old days, I'm younger. And sometimes I'm older.

MOM, *looking at herself:* So this isn't permanent?

DAD: No. But you look great.

MOM: Thank you.

DAD: And it's wonderful to see you again.

MOM: Thank you.

DAD: How are you?

MOM, *she looks around the otherwise empty stage:* Well... if I was alive I think it could be better. And since I'm dead, I think it could be worse. We are dead, yes?

DAD: Yes. Yes.

MOM: Well... *She looks around at the stage again.* Well... I guess it could be much, much worse.

DAD, *also looking around:* Yes. Yes, indeed.

MOM: So this is the next life?

DAD: So far.

MOM: And heaven and hell?

DAD: Yes.

MOM: Where are they?

DAD: This is it.

MOM: Both?!

DAD: Yes.

MOM: Heaven AND Hell?

DAD: That's what I understand.

MOM: Did you ask someone?

DAD: Not really.

MOM: So there could be more?

DAD: Oh yes, there is more. I'm fairly certain of that. I heard others talk... about it. But this is heaven and hell. *Mom goes to her chair and sits.* You look wonderful. *She looks at her hands and nods.* When I saw you it was like the first time we met at Davy's theater...

remember... over on 29th. You were sixteen and so damn cocksure of yourself.

MOM: And you were eighteen and already thinking you were a star.

DAD: Nineteen. And by then I was a star, at least in our little group.

MOM: You had no doubts and I had nothing but.

DAD: I had doubts. All my life has been doubts.

MOM: I realized that later... but at that moment, when I first saw you and you first saw me... I was all shaking pride and you were king of the walk.

DAD: That was my first real home in the theatre. I had spent the summer working in this... this water carnival...

MOM: I remember.

DAD, *to the audience:* The World of Mirth...

MOM: I remember.

DAD: I would put on a deep sea divers suit and get into a tank of water and pretend I was wrestling with an octopus. It was dead but I would thrash around and make it look like it was alive and attacking me. After the show I had to keep it in a jar of formaldehyde.

MOM: I heard this before, John.

DAD, *an angry dog, snapping:* Well, they haven't, so let me finish, dammit. *Back to his story and the audience, falling in love with it all over again.* When the summer was over and I came back to New York, I didn't want to move back with my mom and the kids and I saw an ad in the papers... Butler Davenport was looking for crew for his theatre and he offered a dollar a week and a cot to sleep on. I'd never been to a play in my life... and I walked into the theatre and some actors were dressed up and doing Julius Caesar and Davy saw me and told me to get up on the stage and hold a sword and stand stage left. And so I got up on the stage and... and I looked out at the ocean of seats... and I knew it had to be something special to fill those seats with people and I knew that... that "something" could be me... and from that moment on, I never wanted to get off that stage... whatever it took to be up there.

MOM, *to the audience:* They were holding an open casting for Romeo and Juliet and I went to read for it. *To Dad.* I came in and you asked me what I wanted and I said I was there to read for Juliet and you looked at me and said I wouldn't get it. I remember I wanted to punch you in the nose. And I fell in love with you at that same moment.

DAD: You were stunning... you looked like you were floating... a poem. A fierce poem. I thought you were going to explode.

She sighs at him and at the memory. She looks at her hands, then at him.

MOM: Is Jesus here?

DAD: Haven't seen him.

MOM, *she nods... looks around:* Would have been nice. How about Chopin?

DAD: You know me... I couldn't tell him from Mozart or Beethoven. How are the boys?

MOM: I think they're okay. They seem happy and seem to know what they're doing. Johnny retired.

DAD: Retired? Is he rich?

MOM: No, he's just old enough to get social security.

DAD: Oh.

MOM: I'm worried about him. It was bad enough when he was racing cars and spending all his money on them. *She thinks a long time.* Then he stopped buying cars and started buying expensive wristwatches. Now he's buying all this art. *Like a dirty word.* Picasso.

DAD: The good ones?

MOM: The obscene ones. And he hangs them in his den.

DAD: We couldn't do that in my day. We had to buy books full of all his other stuff just so we could see the few good ones.

MOM: You are his father.

DAD: Well as long as they're real Picassos.

MOM, *bursting in anger:* They're all about fucking. Women spreading their legs and men running around showing off their great pricks…

DAD: What the hell does that mean?

MOM: Don't go there. Don't play dumb and go there.

DAD: Okay, okay. *Thinks of something.* The past is a lie and dreams... the future, is a bigger lie. You know who said that? *She shakes her head.* Johnny.

MOM: I don't believe you. Johnny is a poet. He'd never say anything so dark and sad. When did he say that?

DAD: Now. As he wrote this.

MOM, *agitated:* Something is wrong. I have to go back, he needs my help.

DAD: Elaine...

She gets up and walks quickly around her half of the stage.

DAD, *continued:* Elaine... sit down.

MOM, *calling out:* Johnny! Don't give up hope. You have a beautiful soul, the world needs beautiful souls. You don't have to do anything you don't want to.

DAD: Elaine, stop.

MOM: Just love Alana and keep the two of you happy and be the beautiful soul you already are.

DAD: Elaine.

MOM: Johnny!!!?

DAD: Elaine.

MOM: Did he hear me?

DAD: Many times.

MOM: Can we do anything to help him?

DAD: We did.

MOM: Not enough.

DAD: All we could.

MOM: It wasn't enough.

DAD: No one is.

They both are silent for a while.

DAD: Tell me about Peter.

Mom sighs.

DAD: Tell me.

MOM: He says everything is good but I don't think he knows what he's doing.

DAD: Maybe he does and you won't accept that.

MOM: I'm not telling him how to live his life. I'm tired of hearing that shit from Bernt and you and Johnny and...

DAD: Did I say that?

MOM: You're thinking it.

DAD: You sure?

MOM: Yes.

DAD: Why?

MOM: Because I know you.

DAD: Because you know you.

MOM: Screw you. *He opens his mouth to speak.* Screw you and don't say another fucking word.

DAD, *when he feels she has settled down:* Why do we make something so unpleasant out of something so... so...

MOM: Pleasant?

DAD: Yes.

MOM: Fucking?

DAD: Yes.

She thinks about it and softens.

MOM, *surrenders:* Peter is doing fine. He has this big non-profit place in Malibu and he goes hiking with the Sierra Club and his wife loves him and I guess he's okay money-wise. I'm not sure about the money, but I hope so.

DAD: He's doing better than I did.

MOM: He's smart and he's doing well. I never give him the respect he deserves.

DAD: Did you tell him that?

MOM: No. Is there a way to tell him now, to get word to him?

DAD: He knows you love him.

MOM: I hope so. But I'm not sure. Jesus I hope so… *Calling out.* Peter! Peter... I love you. You are handsome and sweet and I love you and it is only because I have so many things I never got around to doing that I kept nagging you to do more. To be more. But I really love you just the way you are... my little blonde son sleeping on a sandy blanket at the beach and digging holes in the backyard and, and, and I love you Peter and I'll always love you. *Exhausted.* Shit, being dead is awful. *She paces on her side of the stage with agitation.* Right up until the last two weeks or so I told myself I knew exactly how everything was... is. The world and god and the poor and starving and what needed to be done by someone to put it all back on track and dammit if people didn't keep dying and I'd find a way of rationalizing this death and that and I'd think I had put the world back together... and then more sadness and death would jump up and I couldn't sleep at night... because that whole last year I knew something was wrong with me... inside... in my stomach was a lump and I knew it wasn't right and I just didn't want to face it and hear some some... final... final... *She sits and drums her fingers on her knees and doesn't finish the sentence. He takes a worn and folded piece of paper from his pocket.*

DAD: Did you ever read my obituary... that Johnny wrote?

She shakes her head. He unfolds it. She isn't paying attention. He holds it out to her so she can't ignore it. She rises, takes it, and begins reading it to herself.

DAD, *continued, sitting in his chair:* Out loud. It sounds very good... out loud. *Mom looks at him a long time.* Please.

She reads softly and quickly.

MOM: The Hollywood Reporter - March 24th 1992. John Ireland, whose acting career spanned over fifty years and two hundred films, died at the age of 78 of leukemia. Born in Canada, raised in New York's East Harlem, poverty forced Ireland to quit school in the seventh grade. And it was the theatre that became his formal education when he went to work at the Davenport Free Theatre for one dollar a week...

DAD: A little slower... this is a good part.

She looks at him and can't resist a small smile.

MOM: Shakespeare became Ireland's first love and that led to roles on Broadway with Alfred Lunt and Lynn Fontanne. Discovery by Hollywood in 1944...

She stops reading and looks at him. He rises, grabs it from her, and continues reading it... out loud...with more intensity.

DAD: Discovery by Hollywood in 1944 brought Ireland acclaim in a succession of films including "My Darling Clementine," "A Walk in the Sun," "The Gangster," "Red River," and "All the King's Men," for which he received an Academy Award Nomination. *To the Mom.* Remember they said Kirk Douglas and I... both of us got screwed out of our Oscars that year?

MOM: Finish your obituary.

DAD: Did I tell you about the big fight I had with Duke when we were making "Red River"? Monty Cliff and I were stealing the movie from Duke and he was getting pissed off.

MOM: Finish your obituary.

He looks at the obituary... reads it silently... sags... hands it back to her. She reads it as if describing an illness.

MOM, *continued:* A feud with Columbia Studios czar Harry Cohn almost destroyed Ireland's career. But he survived by starring in smaller independent films such as "I Shot Jesse James" and...

He reaches over and takes the obit from her hands.

DAD: And a lot of shit.

MOM: Not all of it.

DAD: Most of it.

MOM: You didn't have to.

DAD: You know what my worst enemy was?

MOM: Your dick.

DAD: Money.

MOM: Your dick was your worst enemy. *She nods at the obit.* Keep reading.

DAD: I don't like the ending.

MOM: It's the same as everybody else's... you die. *He shoves the obit back in his pocket.*

DAD: It was a nice funeral, wasn't it? They played that record I did with Judy Garland.

MOM: The media wasn't there.

DAD: All the seats were filled.

MOM: You didn't make the five o'clock news.

DAD: Screw you. All the seats were filled.

MOM: Not with anyone from that silly book you were writing... not with anyone who worked with you. You know the only one who came up from Hollywood... it was Paul Ross.

DAD: How much did I owe him?

MOM: More than you can imagine... but that isn't why he came to your funeral... he did it because he loved you. You made his life... what... you made it a... a... whirlwind.

DAD: Every time he called me it was to ask when I was going to pay him back.

MOM: And every time you called him it was to ask how much he could loan you. But he loved you, John, he loved you just about more than any other friend you had. And you looked down on him because he was a press agent.

DAD: All right... give it up... shit, you sound like... like...

MOM: Yes. I loved you, too. And you pissed on me, too.

DAD, *to the audience:* I love that scene where Monty Cliff and I... we had just met and we sized each other up by showing off with our guns... and then we traded guns, sort of seeing what the other guy was made up. And then I said...

MOM: What the hell difference does it matter what you said, you fucked it up.

DAD: Me? Hell, it was Charlie Feldman, he was cheating me...

She explodes in anger that grinds into sadness.

MOM: All right, he was cheating you.

DAD: He was my agent, dammit.

MOM: And he was cheating you. So what? That's the way it was... and that's the way it still is. But you fucked up and walked off the picture. You stupid fool. *She points at the audience.* Tell them about the Oscar you didn't win. Tell them about your restaurant that went broke and the book you never finished and how you couldn't pay your taxes and the checks that always bounced. Tell them!

DAD: Okay, okay, okay. It was my fault. It was... my... fault.

MOM: It wasn't just your fault, it's also this... fucking Hollywood, pardon my French.

DAD: Hollywood had nothing to do with it.

MOM: Hollywood has everything to do with it. You're an actor, an incredible actor, and you belonged in New York... on the stage... not getting lost in all that Hollywood trash. You were too damn good for... that...

DAD: Give it up, Elaine... I'm dead.

MOM: I know you're dead.

DAD: God, you were beautiful back then.

MOM: But I wasn't wild enough... like that fat cow you... you... I forgave you every woman but her... I can't even let myself say her name... you slept with that, that, that, that... cow... and I hate you for it. No, I don't hate you... but I don't forgive you.

DAD: You don't forgive me because you still love me. Remember after I left you and married Joanne and I came over to drop off the alimony check and you seduced me?

MOM: Nobody ever seduced you. You expanded beyond all boundaries the meaning of the word available. Yes... I still love who I hoped you'd be. But not who you became...

DAD: It was good enough for everyone else.

MOM: Yes. Yes. But not for me.

He begins walking in circles. She watches him.

DAD: Howard Hawks gave me some of the greatest lines I ever said... and I walked off the picture.

MOM: Okay, okay... move on... so you and Monty finished trying out each others guns and what's the great line Hawks gave you?

DAD: So I hand Monty back his gun and then I size Monty up and see he's still more kid than man, so I say to him, "There's nothing nicer than a fine gun. Except maybe a Swiss watch... and a woman from anywhere. You ever had a... Swiss watch?" *He smiles and shakes his head.*

MOM: Yes... that's a great line.

DAD: And I said it great. At that moment, at the very moment I said that line, I could feel lightning strike me. And five minutes later, I proceeded to screw it all up. Goddammit... why did I do that?

MOM: I don't know.

DAD: Shit... go look at the movie, go look at that scene and you can see what I'm saying. In that moment everyone could see I was a rocket taking off, me, John Ireland, I was the next Bogart and Cooper and Fonda. And it's still there... in those... that... scene... those words... those amazing moments.

MOM: It isn't there, John. You're gone, your life is over.

Dad falls silent. She sits, watches him, and searches for something to offer him.

MOM, *continued:* Daphne misses you. The woman who stayed with you the longest still misses you. And your daughter had a baby, a son. *He turns as if hit by lightning.*

DAD: When?

MOM: A few years ago. They call him Jack.

DAD, *sitting too:* That was my name... Jack... my brothers Mike and Tommy always called me Jack... Jack... it... I... I was different when they called me Jack.

MOM: I wasn't talking about you.

DAD: Okay, okay... so they call him Jack? *Mom nods yes.* Did Daphne remarry? *Mom shakes her head no.* Jack? *Mom nods.* Jack?

His walk becomes as if he was trying on the name.

MOM: Okay, okay... so now tell me about your fight with John Wayne.

He lightens up... enjoys the victory of his story.

DAD: Hell... it wasn't a fight so much as a... a... a... a stupid game. The cast had become two opposing camps. Monty and me were the New York actors, and Duke and his pals were the Hollywood crowd. And Monty and me, we were stealing the show. So one day Dukes calls me over and he tells me I'm walking like a fag... and he tells me... no he starts to show me how to walk. So I look him in the eye and I say "Duke, if I'm going to walk like someone, it will be like Henry Fonda, not you." Well, that pissed him off and we didn't talk after that.

Dad is at last standing straight. He is young again... a star again. He moves down stage and looks out over the audience.

MOM: You loved it. Being famous.

DAD: It was more than I ever had or ever imagined I could have. The New York success seemed so... little... compared to Hollywood. I remember when I got into town... my agent took me to Romanoff's... remember that phony Russian prince... hell, the real royalty were the customers... and Charlie took me there to let me know that I was about to become one of them. We sat as this table and people came by to say hello to Charlie but it was really to get a look at me, to see who the new hot young kid was. And Bogart came by and he looked at me and he said, "Pal, you've got the best new face since ME."

MOM: How did that make you feel? *As he remembers a cloud falls over him.*

DAD: Actually... afraid... like something was going to be expected of me and maybe I'd fail. *He sits there quietly.* I tried to push the feeling away, under the table so no one would see it... in my eyes... hear it... in my voice... smell it on my breath.

MOM: You should have stayed in New York.

DAD: Tommy warned me.

MOM: I warned you.

DAD: Yes... but... Tommy was my brother, he understood me. We used to practice whispering to each other from a half a block away... like we were projecting to the back row of a theater and we had to tell a secret that no one else in the world could hear... except of course the entire audience. We used Shakespeare a lot because it required a sharper tongue and a quicker ear.

MOM: And your brother, Mike? *Dad becomes quiet.* Mike?

DAD: Mike usually wasn't there. He was usually out getting into trouble.

MOM: He loved you. He wanted to be with you.

DAD, *suddenly angry:* Mike was lazy, he never wanted to work for things... he thought it all should come easy.

MOM: Because it was so easy for you and Tommy... you with the acting and Tommy with his comedy. Mike wanted to be like you and Tommy, but he didn't have the talent. And when he came to you for help, you always ran away from him. So did Tommy.

DAD: We didn't run away from him... I gave him work.

MOM: Work?! You treated him like he was your, your... your pickoninny... your lackey... the... the guy who washes your car and picks up the dry cleaning and goes to the bank and makes the deposit that covers your bouncing checks... the guy who in the morning, drives the girls you sleep with home.

DAD: Mike was always looking for the fast buck.

MOM: He was desperately trying to catch up with his brother. He loved you. *Dad can't answer her.* He loved you dammit. And when Tommy was dying, it was Mike who took care of him. Not you, but Mike.

DAD: I was doing a picture in Spain... I got there as fast as I could. Tommy understood.

MOM: Yes he did... and Tommy waited for you to get there before he died... but neither of you said shit to Mike, neither of you ever thanked Mike for being there and taking Tommy for his chemo and making sure Tommy's kids did their homework.

DAD: Mike was a pot head... his own kids ended up just like him.

MOM: And Mike bought you your pot. And he hid your cars from the banks when you got too far behind in the payments. And you'd give him a few bucks... like you were tipping him, for chrissakes! And all the time you wouldn't give him what he really wanted and needed... your love and your friendship. And he'd turn to you and say "Jack... Jack... why are your treating me this way?" And when Mike went to prison, you never wrote to him.

Dad rises to get away, walks downstage. She rises and follows but stays on her side.

MOM, *continued:* You never wrote to him. You know what Attica was like? Of course you don't. But Mike did, he was there. And after he got out, when he was dying in the Veterans hospital with a tumor in his brain, you never once went to see him.

DAD: Stop it, goddammit!

He waves her to stop and she does. He shrugs... looks for some words... almost laughs... almost this and almost that and then he sighs... and he looks at his hands... and he looks at her.

DAD, *continued:* Was it hard for you? Dying.

MOM: Unbelievable. It doesn't let you sleep. It doesn't let you have a simple conversation or go to the bathroom with dignity and quiet... and the heat... the whole last week I was on fire and all I could do was scream for ice to be put all over me. Finally, I was able to shut my eyes and just look at darkness and I could hear everyone fussing and wondering what to do... and there was this one big constant pain and all I could do was moan about it and after awhile my moans and the pain became one and then I think I really did fall asleep... at least it feels that way and then... I was here.

DAD: I felt I was in two places at once... like there was two me's. The one that was dying and the one who was watching me die. Peter was holding my hand and neither of us said anything... well, I couldn't because I was in a coma, but I could see everything. And Peter was holding my hand and then it became very heavy and he had to grab on tighter to keep it from falling. And he knew it at the same time I did. He knew I was dead just at the exact moment I did and then there was only one of me, watching the dead me and Peter. *They both look up at the sky.* Was I a good husband?

MOM: No.

DAD: But I was a good lover.

MOM: You were a sweet lover.

DAD: What the hell does that mean?

MOM: It means just that. You were always very sweet but you weren't the best.

DAD: Who was?

MOM: It doesn't matter and it's none of your business.

DAD: Are you going to ask what I thought of you as a lover?

MOM: No.

DAD: You aren't even a little curious how you compared to the others?

MOM: No. And if you try to tell me, I'll leave.

DAD: Where will you go?

MOM: I'll just start walking and I won't stop until you're not there.

DAD: You haven't changed.

MOM: Who was best?

DAD: Shelly. *Mom nods.* Now you tell me.

MOM: No.

DAD: Why?

MOM: Because you should have lied and said I was.

He suddenly laughs... happily. She joins him.

DAD: I guess this is why they don't let us remember anything when they send us back.

MOM: Yes, we'd be so caught up in the past we wouldn't move forward... the whole experience would grind to a halt.

DAD: What do you want to come back as?

MOM: A man. I want to know what it's like to have this big thing flopping and banging around between my legs.

DAD: Not all of them are as big as me.

MOM: Well I don't know how the hell any of you can walk without giving yourselves headaches.

DAD: You dress right or left. You drop it down one pant leg or the other... and that keeps it out of the way.

MOM: I'll take your word for it but I once tied a banana to a piece of string and tied that to my belt and let the banana dangle between my legs to see what all the mystery was about. I went up and down the stairs once and the poor thing was so bruised it was un-edible. Would you like to see what being a woman is like?

DAD: No... I like being a man.

MOM: Oh, but it's much, much better for us. Look at the sex toys they make. You can buy a perfectly good plastic dick for nine ninety-five and it will do the job anytime you want it. There's nothing on the market for men at that price. You'd probably like sex even more if you were a woman.

DAD: Elaine, stop.

MOM: But this is the way you wanted me to be when we were married. Remember when you and Shelly tried to get me to smoke pot with the two of you? And what about our gay friends... and the bisexuals... Ed and Pamela... now that's the way to go next time. Who do we talk to about signing up for that?

DAD: I don't think it is going to work that way. I think it's more like the subway... they send us down into the station and we all jump on the train and wherever we get out, that's what we get.

MOM: Doesn't sound like they put much thought into it.

DAD: Someone was telling me exactly that... that it isn't as well thought out as we were told... they said it's just another place like the post office. It's a job. No more, no less.

MOM: How disappointing. Worse than disappointing. They really owe us more... we should all make a big fuss about this. *A long beat.* When do I lose all my memories, when do I really die? *He shrugs and shakes his head.* Please tell me it happens fast. The cancer I could take, but I don't want my memories being taken away... leaving me... drop by drop. *A good memory jumps into her brain.* You know what I loved? How you and Bernt liked each other.

DAD: Was he a better husband?

MOM: Yes... he's been a wonderful husband. Life isn't easy and no one is perfect... but he... he... I couldn't have ever asked for more. Ever. And he always brought me flowers. Always. To the very end. Leaving him was the hardest. Just as losing him would have been the hardest if he had gone first. I wish I could see him one more time... just to be a breeze across his forehead. *Neither speaks for several seconds.*

DAD: Remember when we went on tour with Peter Pan?

MOM: You were a wonderful Captain Hook.

DAD: You should have played Peter.

MOM: No... I would've liked to and yet it really wasn't me. Neither was Wendy or Tinkerbell. I was fine being one of the lost boys. And the tour was great fun.

DAD: Yes. Nothing was at stake. We just acted and had... fun.

MOM: You taught me a lot about how to live.

DAD: Tell me.

MOM: Every time we'd get to a new town and check into the hotel, you always found a way to get extra towels and blankets. Once, you even got into another room that no one was using and took some of its furniture. You would fix up your room and you always made sure that your room was... as beautiful as you could make it.

DAD: That's all I really wanted, for life to be beautiful. It just got harder and harder to keep up. Years later... after... us... and after Joanne... but before Daphne... I was doing summer stock and something wasn't right and it was late when I got back to the hotel and I walked into the room and this cold... horror... stabbed me in the heart and I couldn't breathe and I was afraid I was going to rush to the window and jump out. I pushed all the furniture in the room up against the window so I couldn't get to it and then I took a blanket and slept on the floor by the door. The next day I had the hotel move me to a ground floor room. From that night on, I was just waiting to die. From that night on, I just couldn't keep up. I wanted to live forever and yet the simple act of staying alive was getting harder and harder and heavier and heavier. Seventy-eight was too young... way too young... hell, except for the cancer I was in great shape. I was too young... it was too soon... and yet, I was so glad when that last day came and they took me to the hospital and I could hear the talking and I knew I could give it all up and finally rest. *A wind blows across the stage and lifts Mom's hair. They both feel it.* None of it meant anything, did it?

Mom shrugs and shakes her head in uncertainty.

MOM: I guess not.

DAD: It was all just atoms flying about in the universe.

MOM: More or less.

DAD: I just as easily could have been a farmer.

MOM: Well metaphorically maybe... but I don't see you really feeding chickens and milking cows.

DAD: I wrestled that octopus.

MOM: It was dead... you just pretended to wrestle with it. *He thinks about it and shrugs his acceptance of the idea.*

DAD: But I was very convincing.

MOM: I'm sorry you didn't have more fun. *He shuts his eyes and feels her words, then his eyes snap open with a memory.*

DAD: I had great fun when I took Johnny to Europe that summer. What was he... thirteen... no fourteen.

MOM: He loved it. And those beautiful suits you got him at Brooks Brothers.

DAD: You should have seen his face when the steward showed him to his own cabin. Fourteen years old and his own first class cabin on that big French liner, the Liberte.

MOM: In my heart I was with him. He was seeing Europe even before I did. London... Paris...

DAD: The Riviera... Stockholm... one night we were all in Monaco at this famous restaurant. Zsa Zsa was there and David Niven and his wife... myself... Bella Darvi... Larry Harvey... Coop had gone back to

London that morning... none of us knew he had cancer... anyway this Countess had just lost all her money and she made little Johnny be her date... and the whole restaurant broke into this song... everyone was singing it that year... I remember it went Volara... da da... Contade... Da da da daaa. *He looks as if he can see the event.* And we were all singing it and Johnny had been getting some of the wine and his eyes were swimming and he couldn't stop looking at the Countess' breasts... and then he saw me watching him and we both laughed and smiled at each other and... well... it was a wonderful night.

MOM: Thank you for that... his soul needed that trip after what... what happened. I kept watching him afterward... afraid something would go... wrong... to... with... him.

DAD: Me too. But it worked out fine. Later that night, Johnny and I walked back to the hotel and we didn't need to say anything. It was just a beautiful night on a narrow street in Monaco, and I was walking along with my son... and I felt... no, I knew... that on that evening, I had been a good father.

MOM: I was never afraid when he was with you.

DAD: I felt the same about you.

Mom looks out over the heads of the audience and holds up her hands as if shielding her eyes from the sun. Dad stands up. He hums the same brief piece of the song "Volare." Mom sighs and lowers her arms.

DAD, *continued:* I think I'm ready to forget everything and start anew.

MOM: Yes, you're right. I feel it too. Let's hold hands. Like when we met.

He smiles... they step towards each other and for the first time actually touch each other... their fingers embrace... feelings and memories run through them... then they settle down.

DAD: Thank you.

Mom nods and silently repeats the same two words. Dad takes a deep breath and lets it out with a sigh.

DAD, *continued:* Goodbye?

MOM: Of course.

They slowly step backward until their hands are forced to surrender and part.

DAD: The End?

MOM: Or something.

He gives a small wave... steps back. She returns it and does the same. He takes another step back. She does the same. He blows her a kiss. She blows him one. He smiles and turns and walks off stage left. She turns... looks at the audience... a smile whispers across her lips, then she turns and runs off stage right.

CURTAIN

LOOK UP

Sharon Yablon

LOOK UP was first produced by the Padua Playwrights as part of "A Thousand Words," a collaborative evening between playwrights and artists.

CHARACTERS

RICH: *Mid 40s, fatherly and clean cut, but with a false air of self-assurance.*

BELINDA: *Early 40s, Rich's wife. Wears an accessorized sweatsuit. Skittish and pretty.*

DAVID: *Sixteen, Rich and Belinda's son. Contemplative and damaged but hiding it.*

MARLO: *A 50-ish Realtor, she is not shy about who she is. She is dressed provocatively and has a deformity - a visible bending of the body.*

SETTING:

An unfurnished house in a gated community in Irvine

TIME:

The Present

Music in the dark. Lights Up on RICH, BELINDA, and DAVID standing together. MARLO is nearby, in a revealing top. She has a strange disability. The group looks as if they are in mid-conversation and pose.

MARLO: You won't find any weirdoes here.

She moves and her high heels carefully click on the floor. All eyes follow her, and she looks out, with a strange expression.

MARLO: That's reserved for cities. *Pause.* I can't quite explain to you what it's like to see the sun set here. The monotony of the plan, the houses. There is a comfort in living in a house that looks exactly like everyone else's. Or is there? I hope you like this color, puce, because you won't be able to change it. The landscaping is here to stay. The only place to be creative is in your bedroom, perhaps.

She faces Rich.

MARLO: At this time I'd like to know more about you.

RICH: My wife can be insatiable and Viagra can be dangerous. The doctors said that it was the longest time they had seen anybody with an erection. It was my erection.

MARLO: Doctors?! They're a bunch of fools. Didn't you feel powerful, desired? *Pause.* Everybody wants that. My brother is an anesthesiologist at New Samaritan, here in Irvine. You should hear the things he tells me. There's more unexplained coma than you can shake a stick at.

DAVID: When carbon monoxide is pumped into the central nervous system during a surgery, the blood retains its cherry red color. Thus, the attending physicians don't know that the brain has been deprived of oxygen, and is becoming severely compromised.

He looks at Marlo.

DAVID: "Coma" is my favorite movie.

RICH: Don't you want to know how long I had it?

MARLO: You do want your tour, don't you?

RICH: Of course. Although. I can't say I really know what I'm doing. That I've thought things through, you know? Did I choose my path or did it choose me? *Getting scared.* I never imagined I'd work at Hertz. The colors of the office interior, all those people renting cars, in transition. But nothing changes for me. How do people make decisions? What's wrong with waffling? If I never decide anything, what will happen to me?

MARLO: You said you haven't been happy in your house for some time.

RICH: I did? Well, that's true.

MARLO: You should remember what you say and how you feel.

RICH: Okay.

MARLO, *continues the tour:* There's no crime here. That's important and it's not on the brochure.

BELINDA: How can there be a place with no crime?

MARLO: You're right, Lady. There are violent tendencies in all of us. And so I will tell you that people do die here. We have jumpers.

DAVID: Cool.

BELINDA, *a little excited:* Jumpers?

MARLO: Yes.

RICH: Jumpers?

MARLO: Yes.

RICH: Is that a sex thing?

MARLO: People who jump.

BELINDA, *snaps at Rich:* Yeah! *Softer.* I mean, yes, dear.

RICH: Jump?

DAVID: To their deaths, Dad.

MARLO: And if you look around.

Belinda and Rich look around.

MARLO: No, not here! The parameters of the community!

Belinda and Rich slowly walk upstage, look out.

BELINDA: Is that an emu?

DAVID: There really is no need for large flightless birds anymore.
But they must be respected because they hearken back to the dinosaur
era.

MARLO: There's lots of places to jump. The wall for instance, that
runs along the property.

Belinda takes a step towards Marlo.

BELINDA: Was the wall always here?

Marlo gets closer to her and whispers. Rich strains to hear.

MARLO: Are you my strange slut? *Pause, back to her regular voice.* My husband was the developer. I was his girlfriend's friend, and he sized me up like a piece of prey. After I slept with him he became moody and disinterested. He started drawing walls and one day I leaned over and whispered in his ear, if you miss me sucking your penis, you'll tell me what's beyond that wall. He realized that his depression was depriving him of sex, and he drew this whole place, then. A city. Perfect, with its own people and sun. Bright new buildings with no history. Unimaginative plant life. But then he drew these exotic creatures with long, blue necks. And nude people, running all around! Because they had gathered at the gazebo and burned all their clothes! The people wanted to live in the future, so they built monorails. As far as the eye could see, there were nipples and monorails. *Pause.* Oh, the diversity of everyone's body and face! I feel drugged… and there were robots too. Robots who would do anything you want, except be your friend, which is what I really need. I want to make more friends but it's so hard, after college! Anyway. There's no wetlands left in Southern California, so the waterfowl all stop here. Do you have a problem with that?! You're not from somewhere else, are you? If so, are you going to complain and complain about the smog and traffic and lack of aging and beautiful women for everyone to feast their eyes on but never have? Oh, it's abominable here.

BELINDA: We're natives, actually.

MARLO: That's impossible. Even I'm from Colorado.

She approaches David.

MARLO: And what do YOU think of our waterfowl?

DAVID: I like them. What I really like.

MARLO: You can tell me.

DAVID: Is older women. I'll accept any flaw wholeheartedly. I'm sixteen and I need to get as much sexual experience as I can.

BELINDA: David.

DAVID: *It's true, Mom!* Why should we pretend that sex isn't all we care about?

RICH: He's right. I look at you people. You are my family. But are we all ultimately unknowable? Why can't I form a picture of God in my mind? I should have had that threesome in college. It was my only chance. It was happening organically, and I was afraid. I didn't think I'd be able to please two women. And the truth is, one of them was tubby and I couldn't get past that. I'm ashamed. I also realize now, I could have gotten by without touching her stomach.

MARLO: Why on earth would anybody come to Los Angeles? It's poison on the soul. It's fucking beautiful. It's the end of the journey. The land meets the water and there's nothing else. You can relax. Get rid of your toxic personality. Get colon hydro-therapy. *To David.* Girls your own age don't know what they're doing, do they?

DAVID: They really do. But I like Science Fiction, and I need someone I can talk to frankly about it.

BELINDA: I'm an actress! I WILL get an agent, I WILL land a series, and make a successful crossover into film! I will get everything I want!

She glares at Rich.

BELINDA: YOU said that to me when you met me. You said I'm the type of girl who should get everything she wants. My pussy isn't like the others, and I'm funny. Remember that? And so I want it all. Now.

MARLO: Irvine is a hateful place. Don't you know who did this to me?! It was Irvine. I was biking on one of those damned, sculpted bike paths that run through the city, and a car clipped me. I flew through the air and forgot who I was. Then I landed and people gathered around. They cut up my pants leg and I realized that I hadn't yet shaved for the week. They wanted to see where the bleeding was coming from, but I could have told them.

DAVID: Blood trickles slowly down their legs, past their anklets. But her. That woman over there. No longer bleeds. And so, she has more to give.

RICH: Listen to me, women!! I think I've made a mistake with my life. Gone in the wrong direction. That happens to people, doesn't it? I never wanted to be a business major. But I wanted to fuck this girl, Wendy, and she was an accounting major. I lied to her, told her I liked numbers. Zero was my favorite. What is zero, really? I changed my major for Wendy. She had a small round ass that flared out like an onion. I wanted to peel it and forge through it. I'm sorry but that's the truth. *Pause.* Wendy insinuated that she would let me do things to her. I made time, bought lubricants. I could have gone to a semester at sea.

Pause; Belinda looks out.

BELINDA: We used to live in Malibu. We had our own private stretch of beach. I could feel the envy when we went out with friends who lived somewhere else. "What's it like to live in Malibu?" they would ask. Looking out my window. All that beach, stretching out before me. I felt the possibility of my life, what I could do, what there was still time to do. But sometimes the sight of it, the pearl gray water fading into infinity, somewhere at the end of the world… one day there was a big fire. I left my house and went out to the beach. Gradually, the other women came out and we all stood there, silent, on the sand. All the women of Malibu. It was the middle of the day and all our husbands were at work. Some horses had caught fire and came out from the hills and were now on the beach, running, with flames. I had never seen anything like it. The beauty and the horror. And then, I heard a "pop!" I looked around, but didn't see anything. I heard it again, "pop!" *Pause.* Look up! *Pause.* A woman standing next to me said. The birds were exploding from the heat. Feathers and blood floated down onto us. Everything… instantly incinerated. I repeated it to the woman next to me, look up! And we all did.

RICH: You never told me this… why didn't you call me on my cell?

BELINDA: I looked down the line, at all the women of Malibu standing on the beach! *Unsure.* Do we really need men? Couldn't we just, TRY to fuck each other?

THE END

GEORGIE GETS A FACE-LIFT

Dan Guyton

GEORGIE GETS A FACE-LIFT premiered at the Studio Dante Theatre (Michael Imperioli, Artistic Director; Whitney Rank, Managing Director) in Manhattan, NY in September 2004 as part of an evening of one-act plays entitled *DEAR OLD MOTHER... AND OTHER LOVE SONGS.* It was produced by the Incumbo Theater Company (Ethan Baum and Dominik Tiefenthaler, Artistic Directors; Ryan Shrime and Mark Montgomery, Executive Directors). Play was directed by Greg Campbell; set design by Steven Hall; costume design by Ginger Russack; house technician was Rachel E. Connors, and the stage manager was Katherine Vecchio. The cast of *GEORGIE GETS A FACE-LIFT* was as follows:

GEORGIE: *Mark Montgomery*
MOMMA: *Katherine Brecka**
GIRL SCOUT: *Laura Jo Anderson*

* Ms. Brecka appeared courtesy of Actors' Equity Association

Romantic music sets the mood before the play begins. As the lights come down, the music shifts abruptly to a slow and darker piece. The volume rises slowly, but at a steady pace, until the sound is almost deafening. An air-raid siren blares. Then, with a WHOOSH, the lights flash on as bright as day and the sounds all stop abruptly. We see GEORGIE, center stage, seated in a wooden chair, a pistol deep within his mouth. The room is spare, like a small apartment, and the colors are dyspeptic. The chair is the only furniture in the place. There is a doorway in the back, and a window with some blinds. Georgie is a young man, about twenty-four years old. Tears stream down his face, but just as he's about to pull the trigger, the phone on the counter rings. He looks up. He crosses to the phone.

GEORGIE: Hello? *Pause.* No, I've already got long distance. No, I don't want to try it out! I'm happy with my service! *Pause.* No, I don't want caller ID. Thank you very much. Good bye. *He crosses to his chair. He sits. The phone rings again. He crosses to it.* What do you *want*?!? *Quick calm.* Oh hi, Mom. Yeah no, I'm fine. No, I saw it. Yeah, I… I saw the paper. Look, I'm… really busy right now, okay? I gotta go. *He hangs up. He crosses to the chair. He puts the gun in his mouth. The phone rings. He beats the living crap out of the phone.* JUST LEAVE ME ALONE! *He sits down again. He puts the gun in his mouth. The doorbell rings.* WHAT DO YOU WANT?!?

He runs to the door, and flings it open. A GIRL SCOUT is on the other side.

GIRL SCOUT: Would you like to buy some Girl Scout cook –

He shoots her and she collapses.

GEORGIE: Oh god.

He looks around to see if anybody noticed.

GEORGIE: Oh my god, look what you made me do! *He drags her lifeless body into the room then crosses to the door to see if anyone was watching. He slams it shut and locks it.* You never should have come here. I don't even like Girl Scout cookies! *He checks her pulse. There is none. He looks out the window.* Oh Jesus, all I want to do is shoot myself. And I can't even do that right. *He looks down at her.* What are YOU looking at? *Pause.* Yeah, well you're better off this way. Believe me, this life is NOT what you think it is! Just as soon as you feel like you're going somewhere in this world, it just... *Small pause.* It just turns around and bites you in the ass. Trust me, when you get older, you'll s... Well, you know what I mean. So, don't go looking at me funny like I did... Like I did something wrong! Okay? Because I did you a favor! You think I'm a... You think... You know what? I don't care what you think! Because I am sick and tired of all the accusations and the... and the lies. And then feeling like I... I DID NOTHING WRONG! *Pause.* Yeah, that's what I thought you'd say. Just shut up. I lived a good life. I always did everything right. And then, one day it just... *He pulls the chair up to her.* Let me tell you a lesson about life! Okay? Life is not... What do you do? You sell Girl Scout cookies? Okay, let me tell you something. What do you gotta sell? Like 300 of them? Okay. Let's just say you gotta sell, like, 300 Thin Mints, okay? Like you got, okay, you got, like, 300 boxes of Thin Mints, right? Okay, you got 300 boxes of Thin Mints because those are the cookies that everybody loves, right? Okay, so here you are, you're sellin 'em. "Whoop de doo! Buy my Thin Mints!" Right? So, what happens? You sell 300 Thin Mints and what do you get? A medal? A fuckin' PATCH on your shawl that says "Look at ME, I sold three-hundred BOXES of THIN MINTS?!?" Is that what it's for? A stupid PATCH?!? *Pause. He calms down.* Well, that's cool. Because I mean, you know, patches are nice. They add a little color, a little... flavor to your brown and green. But... you just don't understand. You just don't understand that for every patch you receive in life, there will be some mother (*The following word is silent. *fucker**) ready to stab you in the back and steal your patch away from you!!! You just don't understand this. *He cries.* And I'm teaching you a lesson. There will be some mother... You just don't understand. You're just a little girl. *He cradles her.* I had a patch, too, once. You think I'm a monster, but

I had a patch, TOO. It was called a Bachelor's Degree. I thought, "I could own the world." Spent six years in college and I thought, "Man, I finally got it right." Spent six years in c... I finally got it right. I thought, "Now I can get a job. Now I can do something with my life." You think I'm a monster. You think I'm a monster cause I shot you, don't you? You think I'm... Well, I'm not a monster. I only did it cause I care. I only did it cause I... *He stands.* I'm a good MAN. I'm a GOOD man. I'M a good...

He puts the gun in his mouth and roars savagely. He removes the gun and cries.

GEORGIE: Why can't I pull the TRIGGER?!? You're right, I am a monster. They took my job away! What else could I do? I spent six years in college and they took my job away! What else could I do? They stabbed me in the back and took my job away. Just one mistake and they never let it die. Just... one mistake. And they never let it die. I just want my patch.

MOMMA knocks on the door.

MOMMA: Georgie! Georgie! Are you in there?

GEORGIE, *in a panic:* Mother? Mom, what are you doing here?

He tries to lift the Girl Scout, but she is limp within his arms. He drags her around, searching for a hiding place.

MOMMA, *still outside:* Georgie! I've been calling on the phone, but no one answers!

GEORGIE: The phone isn't really working right now, Momma!

MOMMA: Georgie, I know about your job! Are you okay?

He props the Girl Scout up in the wooden chair. He turns to go, but she falls over. He props her up again. He turns to go, and she falls over to the other side.

MOMMA: Open up the door here, Georgie!

GEORGIE: I'm kinda busy right now, Mom!

He grabs the phone cord and ties the girl upright in the chair with it. The door flies open. Georgie aims the gun at Momma. She stands in the doorway, a set of keys in her hand. They stare at each other silently.

MOMMA: I read about you in the papers, George.

GEORGIE: They lied about me, Momma. I never killed no one. *Girl Scout falls to the floor.* Except for her…

MOMMA: You killed a Girl Scout, Georgie?

GEORGIE: She tried to sell me cookies.

Momma stares at him, aghast.

MOMMA: I thought you liked the Girl Scout cookies.

GEORGIE, *sniffling:* Just the Thin Mints, Momma.

MOMMA, *staring at him:* You wouldn't shoot your own momma now, would you, Georgie?

He lowers the gun.

GEORGIE: They lied about me, Momma. They took away my patch.

MOMMA: You can always get it back.

GEORGIE: No! Murder in the first degree! You don't get shit for that. They throw away the key.

MOMMA, *desperately:* You can get time off for good behavior.

GEORGIE, *putting the gun up to his temple:* No! Back off, Momma! There's somethin' wrong with me.

MOMMA: No, Georgie, no! That's how your father died! Please... put the gun away.

GEORGIE: All my life I wanted you to love me.

MOMMA: I do love...

GEORGIE: I wanted you to love me more than you loved him! I wanted you to see that I was TWICE the man that he could ever be! *He falls to his knees.* But, I'm not. I'm a psychopathic killer.

Momma crosses to him slowly.

MOMMA: Oh now, Georgie. You mustn't think that about yourself. You've just made a few mistakes, that's all.

GEORGIE: I KILLED A LITTLE GIRL!

MOMMA: Well, no one needs to know. Come on, I'll help you bury her.

She grabs the body by the leg.

GEORGIE: Momma! The police are looking for me for killing Mr. Meyers!

She drops the leg.

MOMMA: Well, did you?

GEORGIE: Yes! No! I... He took away my patch! I mean, you know, my... my job. He gave it to someone else. Some young upstart in accounting. I... I HAVE A BACHELOR'S DEGREE!!! I just taught him a lesson!

MOMMA: And he never will forget it, will he, Georgie?

GEORGIE: Mom, I've gotta kill myself.

He puts the gun up to his temple.

MOMMA: Georgie!

GEORGIE: I can't survive in prison! They'll rape me in the ass and do all sorts of things!

MOMMA: Georgie...

GEORGIE: Please don't watch me, Momma.

MOMMA: I watched your father die. *He looks at her.* There was nothing I could do. I had just come home from shopping and I heard the gun go off upstairs. I thought it was a nail gun. You know how he was always building stuff. I remember thinking, "God, I hope that's not for me!" *She chuckles sadly.* He was such a thoughtful man. He would always make me things. You know, like that cabinet in the basement? But, then they always looked like shit. I remember thinking, "George McCauley Robertson, if you make me one more wooden birdbath, I will punch you in the face!" But... when I got up there, I... saw your father bleeding on the carpet. He had put the nail gun to his head. I felt the blood rush out of me as his was seeping onto the blue and grey Venetian rug. His last words were, "God this hurts." He never made me anything again.

GEORGIE: I didn't know you saw it.

MOMMA: What?

GEORGIE: I didn't know you saw him… die.

MOMMA, *waving him off:* Oh, I tried to block it out. It still gives me nightmares, though. *She crosses to him, stepping over the body.* Georgie, please don't do this to yourself. I want you to live.

GEORGIE: I killed some people, Momma.

MOMMA: I'm sure that they'll forgive you.

GEORGIE: No! What about their families? She's probably got a momma, too, you know? Someone who doesn't want her to die! Mr. Meyers has a daughter. And a son. And I just killed him. Because he took away my job. People won't be happy, Mom.

Momma folds the Girl's arms into a tea-pot.

MOMMA: Georgie, look! *Singing.* I'm a little tea-pot, short and stout. Here is my handle, here is my spout…

GEORGIE: That isn't funny, Momma!

Momma drops the Girl Scout.

MOMMA, *desperate:* Oh Georgie, you can't take life so seriously! That's what happened to your father. I make fun of one little wooden birdbath and then BLAMMO! He shoots himself with a nail gun. *She crosses away from him.* You overreact to stimuli, Georgie, and that is no way to live your life.

GEORGIE: I need to die now, Momma.

He puts the gun up to his head.

MOMMA: No! Georgie! Tell me that joke you used to tell me! *He looks at her.* The one about the Mexicans.

GEORGIE, *starting to cry:* I need to die now, Momma.

MOMMA: Georgie, please! Just… one more joke for Momma.

Georgie sighs. He lowers the gun.

GEORGIE: Okay.

Momma claps.

MOMMA: Oh, I love this joke!

GEORGIE: What do you get when you cross a Mexican with an octopus?

MOMMA: I don't know! What do you get when you cross a Mexican with an octopus?

GEORGIE: I don't know, either. But, it sure can pick tomatoes.

Momma laughs wildly. Georgie sighs.

MOMMA: Oh, Georgie. You always knew how to make me laugh.

GEORGIE: I need to die now, Momma.

He puts the gun to his head.

MOMMA: Georgie!

Police sirens sound off in the distance. They both react. They stare at each other.

GEORGIE: What?

MOMMA: I... *Thinking.* I loved your father very much. But I hate him too, for what he did. I can't stand to see you kill yourself, Georgie. Not TWO men in my life!

GEORGIE, *whispering:* Momma...

MOMMA: So let ME do it.

GEORGIE: What?

MOMMA: Let me pull the trigger. I... I can't sit idly by while you go and shoot yourself. Not tonight. *Pause.* So let me pull the trigger. I'd... rather hate myself. *Pause.* Georgie?

GEORGIE: Uh huh?

MOMMA: Can Momma pull the trigger, Georgie?

Pause. He nods, childishly.

GEORGIE: Uh huh.

MOMMA: Okay. Then give the gun to Momma now. *Firm.* Georgie... *He gives it to her, slowly, like a child.* Now, that's a good boy. *She holds the gun nervously.* Okay, Georgie. Good boy. Now you close your eyes now, okay, then? And I'll sing a song for you.

He closes his eyes, as she begins to sing. He kneels. She aims the gun at him. The sirens fade throughout the song.

MOMMA: Georgie Porgie pudding pie...
Georgie Porgie close your eyes...
Now it's time for Rock-a-Byes...
Georgie Porgie pudding pie...

GEORGIE: I love you, Momma.

Police lights flash through the room, as if coming through the blinds.

MOMMA: Georgie Porgie handsome guy,
Georgie Porgie say good-bye,
Georgie Porgie time to die.

Georgie's eyes flash open.

GEORGIE: MOMMA!

The blinds give way abruptly, and a spotlight floods the audience with light. Gunshot. Darkness. A body hits the floor.

GEORGIE: God, this hurts.

Romantic music.

END OF PLAY

AMERICAN INTERLUDE

Scott Brooks

AMERICAN INTERLUDE was first performed in New York and Los Angeles and is a Best Play winner at the Nantucket Play Festival.

CHARACTERS

JACK: *30ish. An everyman, more white collar than blue.*

LUCY: *30ish. Girl next door, or maybe someone more exotic looking. Pretty, but approachable.*

THEIR SIGNIFICANT OTHERS

SETTING:

Any Bar, Anywhere

TIME:

The Present

At rise, two couples sit near each other at a bar. Loud music and the noise from the unseen crowd drown out their conversations. They are clearly all in love. MAN from left couple leaves. WOMAN from right couple excuses herself. JACK and LUCY remain. They sit in silence. She sips a glass of wine, he a beer. They glance at each other; look away. Jack looks up at some unseen television screen.

JACK: Go Mets.

LUCY: That would be nice. My boyfriend lives for those guys.

JACK: I'm just a casual observer. Was that your boyfriend?

LUCY: Yeah.

JACK: That's great.

LUCY: Was she...was she your...

JACK: My fiancée.

LUCY: Wow. When?

JACK: Next month.

LUCY: Wow. Congratulations. Good luck.

JACK: Thanks.

LUCY, *pause:* Have I seen you before?

JACK: I live in the neighborhood.

LUCY: That must be it.

JACK: You live around here?

LUCY: No, my boyfriend does. We come in here a lot, though. When I'm in town...I live in Philly.

JACK: Long distance...

LUCY: Yeah...We just started dating a few months ago.

JACK: Because you do look familiar to me.

LUCY: Yeah... there's a very familiar... thing going on right now.

JACK: I noticed it, too.

LUCY: That's good, though. When that happens. *Pause.* I'm Lucy.

JACK: Jack.

LUCY: Jack...Yeah.

JACK: Yeah...

LUCY: What is it about you, Jack?

JACK: I dunno.

LUCY: Hmm...

JACK: I bet you have a dog.

LUCY: I do.

JACK: I bet you have a picture in a frame of that dog you have at work.

LUCY: Wow. How did you...

JACK: You're just a picture of the dog on a desk kind of girl, Lucy.

LUCY: Guess so.

JACK: I like your sweater.

LUCY: Thanks. It smells funny. I bought it in Thailand. *Pause.*
You're a one girl man, aren't you?

JACK: One at a time, anyway.

LUCY: I can always tell.

JACK: That was an easy one. I told you I was engaged.

LUCY: That's what I'm talking about.

JACK: What?

LUCY: You didn't have to tell me that. When I asked you who that
woman was, you could have said girlfriend. You could have said sister.

JACK: Right.

LUCY: But you said "fiancée." Put it right out there. Right away,
made sure there was no misunderstanding. Took yourself out of the
equation. "Spoken for," "Engaged," "Picking out rings."

JACK: I do that sometimes.

LUCY: When?

JACK: To protect myself.

LUCY: Make sure you don't step out of line.

JACK: Oh, yeah.

LUCY: Do you feel like you might step out of line right now?

JACK: Must have.

LUCY: In what way?

JACK: The only way you can when you suddenly hit it off in a bar with a beautiful girl you've never met before. I want to make sure I can trust myself. Because this is one of those times –

LUCY: One of what times?

JACK: This is one of those times when you wonder.

LUCY: Wonder what?

JACK: Nothing.

LUCY: Nothing? Come on! This is life! You were WONDERING! You were wondering, "What's up with this girl?" and "What is this chemistry thing going on here and what does it mean?"

JACK: What is it about the way she holds that glass of wine that makes me want to... I don't know.

The lights begin to change. This is becoming a different moment in time. They are in a different space than everyone else. This is an extreme close up of things never said. Never thought. But they are there just the same.

LUCY: I was wondering too. This is one of those moments, isn't it? "Shit. What if it's you? What if you're the one?" Because there's no way, right now.

JACK: We're both rational people.

LUCY: But I know.

JACK: In my heart.

LUCY: Is it this life time? Or the last? Or the next?

JACK: I know we just met, but...

LUCY: But right now you feel like we just had great sex and you are getting up to get a glass of water and I'm saying, "You wanna watch TV for a little while?"

JACK: My heart is pounding right now.

LUCY: Do you want to have kids?

JACK: We don't even know each other.

LUCY: I would trust you with my life.

JACK: The lives of my children.

LUCY: I wanna fuck.

JACK: I want to go to museums in Europe and see the world's greatest works of art through your eyes.

LUCY: I want to fall asleep next to you on the couch. *Pause.*

JACK: What's your favorite book?

LUCY: "A Farewell to Arms."

JACK: Why?

LUCY: I don't know. I just started saying that whenever someone asked. I read it once and people seem impressed with the response.

JACK: What's it really?

LUCY: Stephen King's "The Stand."

JACK: Me too. You know what book I tell people? "Catch 22."

LUCY: Ha. Good one. *Pause.* My mother would love you.

JACK: Yeah.

LUCY: What do you do? NO! Don't tell me. I like not knowing right now.

JACK : Like when you hear a song on the radio, and it's a good song...

LUCY: Yes, and you don't want to know what the singer looks like?

JACK: Yes, I really like not knowing!

LUCY: I never watch videos. *Pause.*

LUCY: Tell me something you've never told anyone before…

JACK: Like what?

LUCY: I dunno, a secret.

JACK: Uuuummmmm...

LUCY: One time, there was this awful boy in band, this was like the sixth grade, and he always made fun of me in front of everybody because I had really big breasts for that age. He would call me "Nips" and flick my bra strap. I was already so self-conscious about it anyway. So instead of confronting him about it, or sticking up for myself, I suppressed all that rage, like my mother taught me, and broke into the band room and smashed his little clarinet to pieces on the floor. They never found out who did it.

JACK: Good for you.

LUCY: Waddabout you?

JACK: I don't think I have one.

LUCY: Of course you do.

JACK: When homeless people ask me for money I pretend I'm deaf.

She laughs.

LUCY: How does that work for you?

JACK: I don't think they even notice I'm trying. *Pause.* Right now you look like you must have looked when you were a little kid.

LUCY: Why?

JACK: I don't know. I can picture it right now. Like we're freshmen in high school and I want to ask you to dance.

LUCY: Are you shy?

JACK: Yes.

LUCY: Why?

JACK: What if you say "no"?

LUCY: I won't. I really want you to ask.

JACK: I think we should drive cross-country.

LUCY: Order a nice meal.

JACK: Good bottle of wine.

LUCY: Hold my hand. *He looks around.* Please. *He does.* Do you know what I love? I love to sit out on the porch after dinner...

JACK: Our porch...

LUCY: Can you see it?

JACK: Yes.

LUCY: Sit out on the porch after dinner and watch it get dark.

JACK: Some music coming in through the window.

LUCY: Home at last.

JACK: I can smell it on your skin.

LUCY: Let's have kids.

JACK: Boy and a girl.

LUCY: More.

JACK: Whatever you say.

LUCY: I want them all to look like you.

JACK: We'll get a boat, in the summer, I'll come home early from work and we'll go out on the boat.

LUCY: We'll dance at their wedding...

JACK: You'll cry and remember when we were young.

LUCY: We'll be looking through old pictures.

JACK: "Look how skinny you were."

LUCY: "Look how much hair you had!"

JACK: What was that little restaurant?

LUCY: Oh yes, I remember the one. Will you grow tired of me, Jack?

JACK: Will my eye wander?

LUCY: One day you will see that I have grown old and I have given you children, and my body has given up. She will be young and fit. She will make you feel wise and interesting.

JACK: But I still love you.

LUCY: Who is she?

JACK: She's nothing.

LUCY: I haven't been perfect, either.

JACK: I think I know what you are going to say.

LUCY: It was just one kiss.

JACK: How could you?

LUCY: He paid attention to me.

JACK: I was building something. Something for our family. I did it for you.

LUCY: I didn't ask you to. Your daughter doesn't even know you. She needs her father right now.

JACK: She knows where I am.

LUCY: What happened to us?

JACK: Life.

LUCY: No one said it would be easy.

JACK: I didn't make you any promises.

LUCY: Yes, you did.

JACK: What do you want from me?

LUCY: What anyone would expect.

JACK: What is that exactly?

LUCY: Good question.

JACK: I give you my life...

LUCY: And I give you mine.

JACK: What more is there?

LUCY: There is remembering that.

Pause.

JACK: Thank you... for your life. Have I earned it?

LUCY: Yes, you have.

JACK: If that's true, then that's all I could have ever hoped for.

LUCY: If I die first, will you go just days after me from a broken heart?

JACK: Yes.

LUCY: Promise.

JACK: I promise.

Pause.

LUCY: Thanks, Jack.

JACK: So, that's that, I guess.

LUCY: Well, sure.

JACK: You know what? There is something I've never told anyone. I sometimes feel... more and more lately...

LUCY: What is it? It's okay, you can tell me.

JACK: I'm not at all who I appear to be... I mean at work... They have meetings, you know? The other day I was in this meeting with this guy. And I'm looking at him, and he's talking, and I thought, "Who does this guy think I am?" He seemed so serious! I remember the first time I heard myself use the sentence, "Tell them I'm in a meeting!" I almost laughed out loud. But the assistant said, "Fine." I could barely keep a straight face. The whole thing took a second, but thinking back on it now it was the first time I knew I was an imposter. And that I was a good one. Like this guy in this meeting. He was so serious! He cared about his business and he had a briefcase full of papers and stuff to prove it. And I'm sitting there and I must look regal behind my desk... I have my own office; I don't even know when that happened, and I feel like I'm waiting for some director to yell "cut!" So I can jump up and get out of my costume and go home to my real life. But this is this guy's real life. This is this everybody's real life. I'm just doing what I have to, to keep up appearances and live comfortably, but I think some people actually care about the silly bullshit they do every day to earn a living. That is so foreign to me. Sometimes I feel like I am alone in the world just because of that. Just the other day I wanted to yell… I was walking down the street and I imagined standing on top of a payphone and yelling, "I am not one of you! I have no business here! I have no idea what I am doing nor do I care. It takes all of my energy just to act interested! Thank you and have a nice day."

LUCY: Yeah. Maybe you did.

JACK: Maybe.

LUCY: No, I bet you did. You remember it so vividly. Like an URGE that lasted a second but you remember it like it happened.

JACK: A whole separate life imagined as if it were real.

Pause.

LUCY: What would you do?

JACK: When?

LUCY: When you got down off the payphone?

JACK: Live in the woods, build a mud hut, and eat only what I could kill.

LUCY: I don't think so.

JACK: Move to a touristy beach town, open an ice cream stand, earn just enough to get by and read a book a week until I die.

LUCY: First time you saw something you couldn't afford, you'd be right back here.

JACK: Grow a pony tail and join up with a band of ecological environmentalists or something and wreak havoc with evil corporations that pollute the environment.

LUCY, *pause:* Alright. That's cool.

JACK: What about you? What would you do? Stop the ride. Change everything. Different life. Who are you?

LUCY: First chair violin in an orchestra. Stand up comic. Pediatrician.   I would love to write a novel, but I never had a single story to tell. Honestly, if given the chance I would strip, but only once. I would love some important looking technical job on a television set where I order people around and get my own set of headphones and a clipboard. I would love to go to Paris and be a great chef like Audrey Hepburn in "Sabrina." I used to want to be an Olympic... something; figure skater or something. But it seems like a fleeting moment, even if you win, and then what? You know? Or maybe that's the point. Maybe you might as well concentrate on one thing for a while and then move on. Because you're probably going to switch gears anyway. I think the best job in the world would be a travel writer. How do you get that gig? *Pause.* I dunno, Jack. I think I'm lost. I don't know where to go from here. I think I just want love.

JACK: Everyone I know is lost. But you're the only person I've ever met who knows it.

LUCY: Yeah.

JACK: I think that counts for something.

LUCY: Thanks.

JACK: I don't think we ever get the answers to the big ones.

LUCY: Maybe being alright with that is enough.

JACK: Maybe.

LUCY: We're two sides of the same 45.

JACK: It's almost time, isn't it?

LUCY: Listen, You need to hang on to that guy on top of the phone booth. He'll save you one day.

Pause.

JACK: Maybe he'll save us both.

LUCY: I'll always love you.

JACK: I think I always have.

LUCY: Goodbye.

JACK: For now.

LUCY: Shh. Hurry.

They kiss. A kiss that lasts forever and never happened at all. The lights return to normal, the bar ambience returns. They stare straight ahead. Their significant others return and they greet them and everything is as it was.

LIGHTS OUT

RAFT OF MEDUSA-POST MODERN

Christine Emmert

RAFT OF MEDUSA was first performed as part of the Limbo play project for Ohio State University and given a reading as part of the project through Elizabethtown College in Pennsylvania. In addition, it was also selected to be part of the Play Slam at the Last Frontier Theatre Conference in Alaska.

CAST OF CHARACTERS

YOUNG WOMAN: *late 20s*

YOUNG MAN: *late 20s or early 30s, married to Young Woman*

FRIEND: *a man of the same age as the husband*

FATHER TO THE YOUNG MAN: *a conservative man of middle-age, probably Republican*

SETTING:

The back yard of an ordinary home

TIME:

The Present

Lights come up on a YOUNG WOMAN standing on a pile of trash and wood, so assorted as to represent a raft. She is looking out at the audience.

YOUNG WOMAN: I don't see land yet.

YOUNG MAN comes on and dumps some more trash on the pile.

YOUNG MAN: It's garbage. Get off before the trashmen come and haul you away.

YOUNG WOMAN: It's not garbage. I had a vision.

YOUNG MAN: You had a vision last week that my mother would turn into an Indian Deity. It did not happen. Alas. *Pause.* Please come down. It's supposed to start raining.

YOUNG WOMAN, *with a beautific smile*: I know.

YOUNG MAN: Yes. *Pause.* I know you want me to climb up there with you. But that would just be supporting your fantasy.

YOUNG WOMAN: It isn't fantasy. I had a vision. This is the Raft of Medusa.

YOUNG MAN: Not Noah's Ark? That would make sense with the rain on the way.

YOUNG WOMAN: Raft of Medusa. Gericault. This is, of course, the post modern version.

YOUNG MAN: Of course. *Pause.* Is it something I did?

YOUNG WOMAN, *looking out to audience again:* I don't see the land yet.

Enter young man's FRIEND. He is stopped by the sight.

FRIEND: Great installation art.

YOUNG MAN: It's garbage. Hi, Jerry.

YOUNG WOMAN: It's the raft of Medusa. Hi, Jerry.

FRIEND, *to Young Man:* Are you kidding? It's great. Please tell me it isn't garbage.

YOUNG MAN: I tore down the gardening shed.

YOUNG WOMAN: The raft of the Medusa, post modern. Today we have no large sailing ships. Today we have gardening sheds. And when we destroy, we are at sea.

FRIEND: That's deep.

YOUNG MAN: Don't encourage her.

FRIEND: What's wrong with you?

YOUNG MAN: She won't come down. She had a vision.

FRIEND, *eagerly, approaching young woman:* Tell me.

YOUNG WOMAN: Everyone says it's a metaphor. But it isn't.

YOUNG MAN, *yelling:* No, it's garbage!!!!! *Looks at his friend.* I'm sorry, but we were expecting my father any minute now, and you know how he is about…

FRIEND: Metaphors? *Jumps up on the raft-trash pile.* Hey, it's different up here. You can see things. Things you don't usually see from… well, terra firma. Come on up.

YOUNG MAN: No, thanks. I'd rather you both came down.

YOUNG WOMAN: And drowned?

YOUNG MAN: No, not drowned. Help me with lunch.

FRIEND: Hey man, what's wrong with you? You used to have visions all the time.

YOUNG MAN: That was pharmaceutical.

FRIEND: Up here you can see a great ocean. Many ruins of ships. The skies closing over.

YOUNG MAN: Rain is reported. *Gets down on his knees.* Darling, I am begging you. We'll go back to playing games after Dad leaves. I love you.

YOUNG WOMAN: I love you… but this is something larger than sexual desire.

YOUNG MAN: I thought our marriage was something larger than sexual desire.

FRIEND: You don't understand. You don't see. Just climb up here. It IS much greater than any one person. It's survival of the human race.

YOUNG WOMAN: We are floating on an ocean of chaos with the wreck of civilization. This is all that is left. This raft, this moment, this pathetic chance to keep ourselves from the sea gods. The wind is at our back. I don't see land yet.

FRIEND: She's right. The world is awash from here. You are bobbing on the briny waves.

YOUNG MAN: My feet are firmly on the ground. It's my head that's swimming at the moment.

YOUNG WOMAN: When you chopped down that shed you sent a message that our time in the garden was at an end. I don't mean the literal garden.

YOUNG MAN: This IS the literal garden.

FRIEND: She means the garden of Eden. You expelled yourselves from such pleasures.

YOUNG MAN: Don't start interpreting what she meant.

FRIEND: Then climb up here and see for yourself. See what we see from our vantage point. Acknowledge the knowledge of the Eternal Feminine.

YOUNG MAN: That's high talk for someone with a business degree.

FRIEND: You've always looked down on my degree. But what about yours?

YOUNG MAN: Mine? It's in art.

FRIEND: So you should know what the raft of Medusa is...

YOUNG MAN: It's a painting that people took as a metaphor.

FRIEND: And you married a woman with a philosophy degree.

YOUNG MAN, *impatiently:* How many degrees of separation are we talking here?

YOUNG WOMAN: Climb up and sail into the future. Look for the small island where we may procreate.

YOUNG MAN: You're not procreating with Jerry! I'm getting on board. *He climbs up on the pile.* Oh. Oh my. *He looks around.* It's different here.

FRIEND: Didn't I tell you?

They all stand looking out at the audience. FATHER's voice is heard off-stage.

FATHER: Where are you? The gate was opened so I just came around and... *He walks on stage. A conservative man.*

YOUNG MAN: Hi, Dad. I don't see land yet.

FATHER, *after a moment:* I see you tore down that garden shed.

The three of them look at him.

LIGHTS OUT

SHE IS
AND SHE ISN'T

George Freek

SHE IS AND SHE ISN'T was first produced by the Amherst (NY) Players in their 2007 One-Act Festival.

THE CHARACTERS

HAROLD: *A Lawyer, burly, 30s*

CAROL: *His attractive wife, a college friend of David's, 20s*

DAVID: *An insurance agent, thin, 20s*

THE PLACE:

Harold and Carol's living room

THE TIME:

Recently

An expensive living room. HAROLD is pouring himself a drink. DAVID watches him.

HAROLD, *he tastes his drink, smiles:* Perfect! Now, what would you like?

DAVID: Oh, nothing for me. Thanks, anyway.

HAROLD: But I really think you'd better have something. I mean, we're waiting for Carol to make herself beautiful. It might be awhile.

DAVID: You think so?

HAROLD: Oops! I didn't mean that the way it sounded! What I meant was she could keep us waiting awhile. You know women.

DAVID: I'm not really sure that I do.

HAROLD: Now that's a subject!

DAVID: You mean… what I don't know about women?

HAROLD: I mean what does any of us know about them! I'll tell you! I could write a book on what I don't know about them… starting with my wife!

DAVID: Well, if you write it, I'll be happy to read it.

HAROLD: But you wouldn't learn anything from it, because I don't know anything about them.

DAVID, *pause:* You know, I guess I will take one of whatever you're drinking.

HAROLD: Good man! *He pours David a drink.* You know, my father used to have a saying about women.

DAVID: What was it?

HAROLD: I can't for the life of me remember. It was probably rather ridiculous.

DAVID, *smiling:* Then no doubt best forgotten.

HAROLD: My father, in fact, was a rather ridiculous man. Something of an idiot, I'm sorry to say. But yet, he was a GOOD man! In fact, he was really a wonderful man.

DAVID: I'm sure.

HAROLD: Oh yes, wonderful. He was simply a bit of an idiot.

DAVID, *sipping his drink, trying to find something to say:* Well… there are worse faults.

HAROLD: Now my mother! But we don't want to get into her! That would bust your… buttons!

DAVID, *uneasy pause:* Well, look… about this life insurance policy, while we're waiting for Carol, why don't I just fill you in on the salient points?

HAROLD: Oh, not just yet. *He then chuckles with bonhomie.* You know this is a little game Carol plays. This making us wait. She thinks if she takes long enough, I'll get angry.

DAVID: You mean she wants you to become angry?

HAROLD: You know how it works, man! If I get angry, then that shows weakness, and if I show weakness, it gives her the upper hand. You've seen her play that game, I'm sure!

DAVID, *uneasy:* No, not really.

HAROLD: Nonsense, Dave! You KNOW Carol.

DAVID: We simply knew each other… in college.

HAROLD: And she really thought a lot of you. She's told me that.

DAVID: She has? I'm surprised.

HAROLD: Why would that surprise you?

DAVID: Well, I wasn't that important, really.

HAROLD: You think not? *Pause, palsy.* Look, Dave… can I give you some advice?

DAVID: Yes, yes, of course you may.

HAROLD: Well, what I want to tell you is, don't sell yourself short! You have to think of yourself as a unique and singular human being, as an individual! And don't ever forget that. You are IMPORTANT! And tell me this, Dave. Without a sense of your own importance, what are you? Tell me that. *Pause. David looks stumped.* You are UN-important, man! And that's not something you want to be! If you lose faith in yourself, if you suddenly cease to believe in your own importance, well, Good grief! I think you know what that means!

DAVID: Yes, I see what you're saying.

HAROLD: Not, of course, that any of us is really very important in this vast, ice cold universe. But we need to maintain the illusion, don't we? Wow! Isn't that a depressing thought! *He finishes his drink in one swallow.* Listen, Dave, I have to admit I really like you.

DAVID: Thank you, and I, um—

HAROLD: I mean that! You're very sharp! Look, I'll be honest with you. I didn't expect it. Frankly, when Carol told me you were coming over, I blew a gasket! I mean, what would you think? Here I'm expecting this sad sack she knew back in college and who is now reduced to selling insurance! Well, hey... I mean I expected some pathetic sniveling creature, meek as a mouse, begging with his hat in hand, looking for a handout from an old friend because he'd fallen on bad times. That was my expectation! Do you blame me?

DAVID: Um... no, I suppose not.

HAROLD: But then I find you! Confident, sure of yourself, in command of the situation—

DAVID: Right! So then, about this policy—

HAROLD: Whoa! Now let's not push it, Dave. I mean, I like a man with self-confidence and drive, but that sort of thing can go too far. I think there's something to be said for good old-fashioned courtesy. And if you're the man I think you are, you'll agree with me on that.

DAVID: Yes, I do. In fact, if I can say it, my father used to have a saying about courtesy—

HAROLD, *interrupting, he pours himself another drink:* So you remember your old man, do you? I find that admirable in you, Dave. My father was a wonderful man himself. He drank a lot. In fact, he drank like a fish. It caused us some rather embarrassing moments now and then. In fact, just between us, I once tried to kill the old devil. Of course, it was really my mother's idea. But it never got off the ground. Thank heaven for that... because in the end, old pop was really a pretty decent sort. In fact, it was really Mom I came to loathe. *He takes a large drink.* I think I actually could have done her in a second. By the way, I'm embarrassed to admit that. And I did learn a lot from her. She was a Professor of Law, at a major university. But what she really taught me about was women! I learned all about womankind from that old... *He notices CAROL enter...* That old... mom of mine! Well, here she is! *He kisses Carol.*

CAROL: Hello, everyone. Mmm, I think I'll have one of those, all right? *Indicates drink.*

HAROLD: All right! Another martini! *He mixes it.*

DAVID: Hello, Carol. Well, I see I don't need to ask how you are. You look wonderful!

HAROLD: Doesn't she.

DAVID: I mean, you haven't changed at all!

CAROL: Well… it wasn't that long ago, David.

HAROLD: She hasn't? *Handing Carol her drink.* So tell me, sweetheart, has Dave changed?

DAVID: Oh boy, I'll bet I have.

CAROL: Well… yes, actually, I'd say he has.

HAROLD: He has? How has he changed?

CAROL: Well, if I can be honest, I find it odd he's selling insurance. I mean we all thought David would become a famous artist. He was bright. He was talented. He was sensitive—

HAROLD, *a 'gestured' elbow in David's ribs:* Well, well, so old Dave was 'sensitive', was he?

DAVID: No. No. I mean, I wasn't all THAT sensitive.

HAROLD: Now, don't be ashamed of it. If I may, I'd like to say something about this sensitivity business. As a lawyer, I think I know something about it. I mean, I have to deal with clients! They are human beings, you know! And they are often human beings in emotional distress. Now, I have to minister to their emotional distress, so I can tell you I have learned something about this sensitivity crap!

DAVID: Well, as a matter of fact, I did go to art school for a couple of years. But in the end, I had to give it up.

CAROL: Oh my. I think that's a terrible shame. I mean, it's just a terrible waste of all that intelligence and talent and sensitivity. Why did you leave?

DAVID, *pause:* Actually, there were many factors involved. *Carol frowns.*

HAROLD: Oh boy, now I'm afraid you've upset her, Dave. *To Carol.* You know what? You probably need another drink. *He reaches for her glass and knocks her drink all over her.*

CAROL: For Heaven's sake! Look what you've done, you boor!

HAROLD: Oh boy, I'm really sorry, sweetheart!

CAROL: Will you please excuse me! *She exits.*

HAROLD: Wow, that was clumsy of me! I feel like an idiot! I wish you hadn't upset her, Dave!

DAVID: I'm sorry. I'm really very sorry. But listen, Harold... Um, May I call you Harold?

HAROLD: Yes, of course, Dave! What else! *He winks at David.*

DAVID: Well, look, I was just wondering, do you think we could discuss the policy now? I mean, it's clear you love your wife very much. You are thinking of taking out a very large life insurance policy to provide for her if... God forbid, anything should happen to you!

HAROLD: You're right, Dave, I love her very much. I mean, she is beautiful, she is charming, she is caring, and she is witty! Who wouldn't love her, right?

DAVID, *wary:* Well, yes, from what I know of her.

HAROLD, *he takes a long drink, looks at Dave:* Of course, as you know, she has her faults.

DAVID, *laughing nervously:* Well, they say no one is perfect.

HAROLD: I know, but these are rather serious faults, I'm sorry to say.

DAVID: No. Now I think you're putting me on.

HAROLD: Oh yes, Dave. In fact, when I first met her she was something of a… tramp.

DAVID: What! Now I know you're putting me on!

HAROLD: You don't know? I'm afraid there's no other way to put it. Back in those days she gave a tumble to anything in pants. You wouldn't believe some of the creatures she… took to! In my opinion, some of them were barely human! Naturally, it upset me greatly. The thing is I couldn't understand why such a lovely, charming woman would waste her time, much less become… intimate with such miserable specimens of humanity! Naturally, I had to ask myself why, and do you know what I came up with?

DAVID, *chuckles, very uneasy:* I still think you're just putting me on, Harold.

HAROLD: I decided it was pity! That's right. I decided she must feel charitable toward such pitiful creatures. But I also felt that charity had its limits.

DAVID: I... you know, I really find all this kind of hard to believe, Harold.

HAROLD: Oh, but the story has a happy ending, Dave.

DAVID: Aha! So you are just pulling my leg, after all.

HAROLD: Oh no. The happy ending is that when we married, all that... trouble... ended. The joy of married life, of married life with ME, if I can boast a little, cured whatever it was that caused her... promiscuity. You might say, if you'll excuse the vernacular, that I scratched her itch. Yes, that's right, Dave, our happiness is now such that I can safely say she has never since felt the desire to roam.

DAVID: I'm glad to hear that, Harold, and if I may say so, you're a lucky man.

HAROLD: Yes, I am, and how about you?

DAVID: What do you mean?

HAROLD: Well, you just mentioned how lucky I am with Carol. How lucky are you?

DAVID: Oh. You mean my love life? Actually, at the moment, the girl I've been seeing... Well, we're temporarily not seeing each other. But I'm confident things will work out.

HAROLD: Don't get too confident.

DAVID: No?

HAROLD: Oh no. To become over-confident is to lose sight of reality, and you never want to lose sight of reality, Dave. Let me tell you! I once knew a man who lost sight of reality.

DAVID: Did you? *Pause.* What happened?

HAROLD: Well, he lost sight of reality, so I lost sight of him. But what I HEARD of him was sad. In fact, I heard some very ugly stories about him, and that was truly sad because at one time he was a handsome and ambitious young man. In fact, something like you today.

DAVID: I appreciate that compliment.

HAROLD, *he finishes his drink:* And now let's have another drink!

DAVID: I, uh, haven't finished this one yet.

HAROLD, *a bit drunk:* Look, I would like to tell you something, Dave. I feel that sharing drinks is more than simply being sociable. I feel it is necessary to make the social exchange even possible. You understand me? I mean, it brings out our better emotions. It almost has something mythical about it. Now heaven knows I could be way off base on this. I mean, I haven't actually read a lot of anthropological STUDIES on the subject, so maybe I am terribly wrong? I'd like your opinion here.

He looks at David.

DAVID, *finishes his drink:* Well, I don't suppose one more could do any harm.

HAROLD: Then you agree with me? Good! *He takes David's glass and re-fills it.*

And then Carol re-emerges. She is wearing an entirely different outfit.

CAROL: I hope I didn't take too long.

HAROLD: Well, it was worth the wait, sweetheart! You look stunning, doesn't she, Dave?

DAVID: Yes, very nice.

CAROL: I hope you're not just saying that.

DAVID: Well, now that we are all finally here, maybe we can get down to business. *He opens his briefcase.* Now, about this policy—

HAROLD: Oh boy! Wouldn't you know it! Now I have to go pee pee! Will the two of you excuse me for just a sec? *He exits rather unsteadily.*

CAROL, *she mixes herself a drink:* Well, now you have met the man I married. What do you think of him?

DAVID, *pause:* I like him.

CAROL: You do? Why is that?

DAVID: Well… he seems to have a pretty strong personality.

CAROL: Yes, that's what I thought when I first met him. In fact, that was WHY I married him. I thought he could protect me.

DAVID, *in spite of himself:* Protect you… from what?

CAROL: Oh boy… from everything! What was I afraid of? I can't say. I was simply insecure. You probably know that. But I believed Harold was strong, and he could protect me from… whatever. The problem is he's not strong. In fact, he's actually rather weak—

DAVID, *uncomfortable:* I don't see that.

CAROL: I'll tell you what I feel for him: pity. Basically, I pity him. I find him pitiful.

DAVID: Well, all right. And compassion is a wonderful quality. God knows we all need it. But I'm assuming, since you married him, you must also have loved him.

CAROL: But tell me, David. Do you have any idea how lonely feeling such pity can make one? I'm telling you this because I think you can understand it. You have a deep capacity for understanding, and that's a wonderful quality, a rare and beautiful quality! *Nearly sobs.*

DAVID: No, no! Look, Carol, I don't think you really know me.

CAROL: Oh, I'll bet that I do, David. *She goes over and puts her hand on his arm.* I'm sure I do.

DAVID, *walks away:* No! You don't! I mean all this sensitivity stuff! Do you know why I went to art school? I thought I wanted to express myself, my INNER self! Well, I tried, but I discovered I really had no inner self to express! At least no inner self worth expressing! Of course that upset me, but I got over it because when I looked around, I realized most of my fellow 'artists' were as vapid as I was. They just didn't seem to know it—

CAROL: David—

DAVID: No! I'm not finished. You might say by admitting that to myself, it made me superior to them, but what I'm really saying is that you couldn't possibly know me, Carol, because there's hardly anything, hardly anyone to know!

As Carol goes and puts her hand on David's shoulder again, Harold appears. She may or may not notice Harold. David does not.

CAROL: David, darling, I think you're being far too hard on yourself.

He turns and looks at her. And they both see Harold, as he re-enters the room.

DAVID: Oh good. Here's Harold. Now maybe we can get down to some serious business.

HAROLD: No! Just a minute here, Dave! I have the feeling I missed something. Yes, I really feel like something happened while I was... away for a minute.

DAVID: No, Harold, nothing at all happened. We were waiting for you so we could begin.

HAROLD: Oh no, Davey! You know what? I think I missed you coming on to my wife!

DAVID: What! That's ridiculous!

CAROL: Oh no! *To David.* I'm sorry, David. He's terribly jealous. *To Harold.* For heaven's sake! Please try not to make a fool of yourself... again.

HAROLD: Me? ME! What would you expect me to do, my dear! Here I find Davey-boy coming into my house on the pretext of selling me a gigantic life insurance policy, a million dollar life insurance policy! And then behind my back he abuses my hospitality! He tries to make love to my wife!

DAVID: What! No! Harold, you can't believe that!

HAROLD: No? Now you listen to me, Davey! Just because she... you... had her once, out of some misguided sense of PITY, don't think you can get it again! *To Carol.* Now listen, my love, there are a few things I've learned about Davey that I think you should know! For one thing, he didn't quit art school! He flunked out! He couldn't make the grade—

CAROL: He was just telling me that, Harold.

HAROLD, *somewhat taken aback:* Oh. Well, something else! Did Davey tell you he is a drunk! That some little tramp he was shacked up with gave him the bootheel because he is a falling down, heave-your-guts-out drunk? And so he doesn't have a dime to his name. He's flat on his back broke! Isn't that so, Dave? *He goes over to an ornate vase.* Now let me show you something about me, Davey! See this little trinket! *He picks up the vase.*

CAROL: For God's sake, Harold! Be careful with that! It's an original Roberto Domingo!

HAROL: Is it? So how much is it worth?

CAROL: At least ten thousand dollars!

HAROLD: Perfect! *He smashes it.*

CAROL: Harold!

HAROLD: It's all right! Go buy ten more!

CAROL: That was really obnoxious!

HAROLD: Look! I just wanted Davey to know he couldn't get away with seducing my wife!

DAVID: But, it's not true!

CAROL: Oh, forget it, David. I'll tell YOU something now. He probably wanted you to seduce me.

HAROLD: What! What did she say! What!

DAVID: Look, I think I'd better leave now—

CAROL: No! He brought it up, so let's get it all out! He has become a pathetic, half-impotent voyeur, so you certainly can ignore his ridiculous and crude insults—

HAROLD: No. No! That is not—

CAROL: Oh shut up! *She looks at the vase.* Do you realize what you have done! Do you realize what a FOOL you have made of yourself! Well? Do you, Harold? DO YOU!

HAROLD, *instantly crushed:* But… I didn't mean… I mean, I really truly thought…

CAROL: Apologize! Go on! Apologize to David! *Pause.* IMMEDIATELY!

HAROLD, *whimpering:* But I… I thought…

DAVID: It's okay, let's forget it. It's all right—

CAROL: NO! Harold! DO IT!

HAROLD, *nearly in tears:* Well, I… I'm sorry, Dave… I mean if I was wrong…

DAVID: Look, I really think I should just leave now.

CAROL: NO! Wait a minute. Where is that policy? *She sees it on the table, picks it up, and hands it to Harold.* Now sign it! Go on! That's the least you can do! *Tearfully, he does. Carol then hands it to David.* Here you are, and I'm terribly sorry, David.

Rather stunned, he takes the policy, starts to exit, then turns back.

DAVID: Look, I would just like to make one thing clear. There was only the one time, and it was many years ago. Carol had been on a date with someone, and afterwards she stopped by my place. She was very upset. It seems this person she was out with, and I think it was someone she cared for, he had been rough with her. I think he even struck her, and so she was very upset. But all she really wanted was a little comfort, and so I comforted her as best I could. Then somehow, by accident really, that turned into something more. I mean, she was just very sad and very hurt and she had come to me for comfort, and so I gave it to her. That's all it was. And until this moment, we had never spoken of it again. *David then exits.*

CAROL, *after a pause:* Well… that was unpleasant! I want a drink!

HAROLD: Carol, listen, I'm so sorry. I am truly very sorry…

CAROL: What a night! Well, I am going to have another drink! *She pours herself one, taking a big drink from it.* THAT doesn't even help!

HAROLD: Please! I just want to say one thing. If I made a mistake, it's only because I love you—

CAROL: Harold, I don't want you to say anything more. Do you understand? I'm suddenly very tired, and I am going to bed. Good night!

HAROLD: No! No, you can't go to bed yet.

CAROL: Don't be ridiculous! Of course, I can.

HAROLD: Do you want me to beg, Carol? Is that what you want?

CAROL: No, Harold, I don't. I just want to go to bed. That's really all I want.

HAROLD: Please, wait one minute. There's something I want to tell you. Please. This happened when I was just a kid, eight or nine. I had this friend. I felt very close to him. He lived a few blocks away, but I used to go out of my way to walk to school with him every day. And for a couple of months, we did everything together. I mean, we played ball together. We went to movies together. We spent the night at each other's houses: all of the things kids do with their best friends! I mean, I can honestly say I loved this kid, as one kid loves his best friend. Then one terribly cold winter evening as we were walking home, he suddenly turned and pushed me into a snow bank. For no apparent reason! Then he laughed in my face and ran off to play with some other kids. Well, I didn't know what to think. Of course, I was shocked. And I was terribly hurt. But then, slowly, it began to dawn on me. This friend I thought I had loved didn't actually care about me. It seems he didn't even LIKE me! He'd just… used me! And so I began to cry. And sometimes, when I think about that, I still cry. *Pause.* What I'm trying to tell you, Carol, is that I love you. If I made a mistake, I'm sorry, but I do love you, very, very much! So I'm asking you to forgive me. Do you think you can do that? Really, I'm begging you, Carol. Can you forgive me?

He stares at her. She walks off and stands at a distance from him, standing on the other side of the room, her face averted from Harold, as the lights slowly fade to A BLACKOUT, and…

THE PLAY IS OVER

AMARILLO ROSE

David Miguel Estrada

AMARILLO ROSE was workshopped by First Stage Hollywood at The Hollywood Court Theatre.

CAST OF CHARACTERS

JOE: *An aging military man, sixty-something*

JOHN BOY: *Joe's son, twenty-something, young and restless*

ROSE: *Young, beautiful woman; John Boy's fiancée.*

SETTING:

South Texas

TIME:

The Present; Winter

Lights Up on a small, cramped trailer. There is hardly any room to move around with all the beer cans, bottles of liquor, and various products made in China, assembled in the USA, bought from the local Wal-Mart. JOE, a sixty-something old man sits in a Lazy-Boy chair, shining his shotgun. His wizened eyes hint of a hard life in the military. A.M. news radio blares. There is a knock at the door.

JOE, unsure: Hello?

There is a longer, sustained knock.

JOE: Alright. Alright. Hold your horses.

He unlocks two bolts and opens the door. His son, a tall overgrown young man, JOHN BOY, stands next to him, dwarfing him for a brief moment. Joe, seeing that it's his son, walks quietly back to the recliner.

JOHN BOY: Hey, Pop. So what's shakin'?

JOE: My knees and every other part of my body. I'm a veteran. What kind of question is that?

JOHN BOY: Oh…

JOE: What you been doin' with yourself?

JOHN BOY: Just workin'.

JOE: That's good. Work's good…

There is a long, uncomfortable silence.

JOHN BOY: Well…

JOE: Well…

JOHN BOY: Well…

JOE: Yeah?

JOHN BOY: Well, I just came down to tell you I'm gettin' married.

JOE, *suddenly interested:* Married? Married to who?

JOHN BOY: A girl…

JOE: I figured that much. What's her name?

JOHN BOY, *smiling:* Rose.

JOE, *taking it all in:* Where'd you meet her?

JOHN BOY: At the bus station in Amarillo!

JOE: Texas?

JOHN BOY: Yeah, Amarillo Texas! Where do you think?

JOE: Well, that's more than a little strange…

JOHN BOY: Why's it gotta be strange?

JOE: You might as well of met her at the inner' net...

JOHN BOY: No, it ain't. Nothing strange at'll. You met Ma when she was hunched over puking her head off at the State Fair!

JOE: You get your stories mixed up, boy.

JOHN BOY: No, I don't and there's no refutin' it.

JOE, *annoyed:* We met at the State Fair, yes... that part's true.

JOHN BOY: Well, there you have it.

JOE: But there was no hunching over. That part's nothing but…that's fabrication that your Auntie Christina made up. Your mother had a few drinks, yes. That's true enough. *Suddenly very annoyed.* Why do you bring that up anyway? What's that got to do with anything?

JOHN BOY: I'm just kiddin'. You know how it happened. I met Rose at the bus station!

JOE: In Amarillo...

JOHN BOY: That's right. In Amarillo!

JOE: What was she doing there?

JOHN BOY: She was waitin'.

JOE, *suspicious:* Waiting for what?

JOHN BOY: Well, what do you think people wait for at the dag-gum bus station? The bus! She was waiting for a bus! Dag-gum-it, I swear!

JOE: You never know. She coulda been waitin' for the next John to walk up to her. Who knows who she could have been waiting for? These days...you never know for sure.

JOHN BOY: Pop, you're one sick sum-of-a-bitch, you know that?

JOE: I'm just being realistic. There ain't nuthin' in life for free. You gotta be careful these days. Gotta remember to wear them jimmies...

JOHN BOY: Nobody calls 'em that anymore!

JOE: What?

JOHN BOY: They call 'em condoms!

JOE: I don't care what you call 'em. You put 'em on. Then again, I take that back. I want a grandson yet. Now that you're married...

JOHN BOY: Why?

JOE: What do you mean why? Can't an old man want a grandson? Is that so wrong? I want you to carry on the good Baird name. I want you to carry it like a torch for future generations to say "Hey all you dipshits! The Bairds lived! And they populated. In some instances, overpopulated."

JOHN BOY: You're losing your marbles.

JOE: Well, maybe so. Wouldn't you... wouldn't you if you went through what I went!

JOHN BOY, *correcting:* Through... wouldn't you if you went through what I went through.

JOE: Don't you finish my sentences!

JOHN BOY: You can't talk like that! You can't leave a sentence open-ended like that!

JOE: Like hell I can't! I fought in two world wars. I can do whatever the hell I want.

JOHN BOY: What'd I tell you about that?

JOE: Now you listen to me, Son. Just cause you finished high school and got educated don't mean you gotta throw it in my face!

JOHN BOY: Shit. I ain't throwing nothin' in nobody's face. I just came here to pay my respects.

JOE, *offended:* Do I look dead?

JOHN BOY: You really want me to answer that?

JOE: You gotta real smart tongue, boy! I knew a smart guy like you in the Marines. He died! Friendly fire...

JOHN, *pause:* What's that suppose to mean?

JOE: Nothin'. I'm just telling it like it is.

JOHN BOY: You're crazy.

JOE: Call me crazy. Just don't call me lazy. I fought in two world wars.

JOHN BOY: You fought in Vietnam and Korea. Last time I checked them weren't world wars!

JOE: Well, the world was watching...

JOHN BOY: It don't count that the world was watching.

JOE: You listen to me, Junior! Don't be pissing on my legacy! This is my house and I fought in two world wars! I don't care what you say about your Mama, but don't you come into my house and start in on me! You know, Dr. Phil told me I gotta cut that shit outta my life.

JOHN BOY: Dr. Phil? Who the fuck is Dr. Phil?

JOE: You better watch your tongue, boy! You ain't too old to get some sense knocked into ya!

JOHN BOY: Okay. Who's Dr. Phil?

JOE: That's better. Doctor Phil's a television personality... on TV, dummy!

JOHN BOY: Television personality? You mean that old guy with the goofy lookin' moustache?

JOE: That's him. He's a bona fide doctor. He ain't no crackpot. He knows his stuff.

JOHN BOY: Well, how the hell did you talk to him?

JOE: Purely coincidence.

JOHN BOY, *excited:* Were you on TV?

JOE: Don't you think I woulda told you if I was gonna be on TV?

JOHN BOY: Well, don't keep me in suspense. How'd ya meet him?

JOE: He just happened to be at the book fair... signing his book! And it was there that I thought to myself what better place to ask a medical question. I said, "Dr. Phil... Joe Baird. I seen you on the TV show and I appreciate what you do."

JOHN BOY, *giggling:* You said that? I appreciate what you do? *Joe shoots his son a cold stare.* I'm sorry. I'm listenin'.

JOE: Listen for once in your life. You'll learn something. Life is nothin' but a psychological chess game, son. I knew if I complimented him he'd be more inclined to hear me out. So... after that... I said, "Dr. Phil, I've gotta a problem." He said, "What's your problem, Joe?" I said, "Well, sometimes my heart starts racing and my chest tightens up a bit. On these certain occasions I find it difficult to breathe." He said, "Joe. It looks like you got an anxiety problem." He said, "Whatever you got in your life that's causing you stress, you gotta get rid of it!"

JOHN BOY: That's what he said...

JOE: That's what he said. *Bluntly.* And son... you're... stressful.

JOHN BOY: What do you mean I'm stressful?

JOE: I mean you stress me out.

JOHN BOY: Ah, everything's my fault isn't it?

JOE: Look, I ain't never been one to sugar-coat things, son. But, to tell you the truth, you're my number one stress right now. *Pause.* And I don't like you comin' in and opening the winders at odd hours of the night!

JOHN BOY: Once! It only happened once! Three years ago!

JOE: Well, once is enough. Once is too much. Now I can't go to sleep. I toss and turn wondering if you're gonna come again. Or sometimes I hear something and wonder if it's someone else come to get my stuff.

JOHN BOY: All due respect, Pop, you ain't got much stuff to take.

JOE, *pointedly:* You been casin' the place?

JOHN BOY: What do you mean?

JOE: How the hell you know what stuff I got in here?

JOHN BOY: Well, from what I see, there ain't much stuff.

JOE: Well, now you got me wonderin'.

JOHN BOY: What, you got some stuff hid in here or what?

JOE: If I did... what the hell would I tell you for? I'm warnin' you, son. You better stop asking me so many questions. I'm sick and tired of you comin' here like Custard and his men askin' me all sorts of questions.

JOHN BOY: I don't mean any harm, Pop. Golly... I just don't want you hoarding up things in here. I mean, you're practically a dead man with a pulse. What are you gonna do with all your stuff?

JOE: You get the hell out of here with that kind of talk, you good for nothin' lousy son of a bitch.

He picks up a shoe and throws it at John Boy but misses.

JOHN BOY: Hey!

JOE: Hay's for horses, you sum-of-a-bitch! I'm your father. You're supposed to call me sir! You're supposed to treat me with respect!

JOHN BOY: I don't mean any harm, Pop!

JOE: Well, Hitler didn't mean any harm either, did he?

JOHN BOY: Sure he did. You mean to tell me that planning a master race is good intentions?

JOE: He meant good for his country!

JOHN BOY: Yeah, but—

JOE: Ah, shut up! Hitler was a tyrant but he had good intentions.

JOHN BOY: I don't know how killing Jews was good intentions—

JOE: Not that part! God damn it! Now I forgot my point. You get me off track!

JOHN BOY: I'm just saying...

JOE: I heard you out. All your fuckin' life... I heard you out. I'm beginning to think it was all a waste of time.

JOHN BOY: How could you say that?

JOE: Easy... All that time I spent rearin' you, I coulda been fishin'.

JOHN BOY: You coulda been fishin'...

JOE: That's right. Fishin'.

JOHN BOY: Wow...

John slumps in his chair. The sound of a DOOR KNOCKING. Joe sits up in his chair and finally moves to the door to see who it is.

JOE: Who in the Sam Hell could that be?

JOHN BOY, *monotone:* That's my fiancée.

JOE, *looking out the window:* Hmmm... pretty girl.

JOHN BOY: She's okay.

JOE: What she want with you?

JOHN BOY: I don't know. Says she loves me. Well, aren't you gonna open the door?

Joe scratches his head.

JOE: I wasn't really expecting no company. Let me tidy up a little. *Joe throws a few magazines in the trash. Another knock. Joe opens it amiably, trying his best to make a good impression.* Oh, hello!

ROSE: Are you John's father?

JOE: That's right. That's me. John Boy's father. That's all I've ever aspired to be... In fact I stopped aspiring after he was born... just kidding, but partly true.

ROSE: Is he here?

JOE: Oh, sure he is. He's sittin' down right over here... restin'.

She turns her head to see John sitting on the recliner chair in disappointment.

ROSE: Is everything okay?

JOE: Oh, everything's fine. John Boy here is just tired from the trip.

ROSE: Oh. Are you okay, honey? You don't look yourself.

John shakes his head.

JOE: Go ahead and sit down. Now how long was the trip? Go ahead and pull up a chair. Here, have mine.

He fixes her his chair. She sits.

ROSE: Oh, thank you.

JOE: You want some tea or lemonade?

ROSE: Well, I don't want to trouble you.

JOE: No trouble at all. I got some here. What'll it be?

ROSE: Lemonade would be great, thank you.

JOE: Lemonade it is. *He hands it to her.* That's good. That's good. Drink it all up. There you go. Eh hmm... so! Well, here you are! So damned cute! Look at you. All woman! Good job, John Boy. Very good job! John Boy's young and virile! He's got all the best genes. He played football in high school. Did he tell you that?

ROSE: No. I mean… yes. He mentioned it.

JOE: They were almost State Champions. Tell her the story, Young John.

JOHN BOY: Yeah... we were almost State Champions.

ROSE: Oh… That's nice.

JOE: You're gonna marry him and you didn't know that?

ROSE: Well, no.

JOE: Seems like something he might of said. Might of spoken about more than just in passin'. Right, John Boy? Why didn't you tell the young lady your almost State Champions story?

JOHN BOY: I don't know. It just didn't occur to me.

JOE: Just didn't occur to you? John Boy doesn't like to toot his own horn. He likes to keep it all under wraps. Like this visit here. Surprise! Comes on me like a thief in the night like that pulling his car into the driveway. That's how he is. Never know what he's going to do next. Isn't that's right, John Boy! See there. He don't tell his old man nothin'. That's how he's always been. When he was a child he'd just sit in his stroller and make a wild-eyed look like he was Manson himself. Look at the pictures! See for yourself! Didn't look like any Baird I'd ever seen. But he grew to be good natured. Fairly good natured. Got it from his mother's side, God rest her soul. Anyway, that's how he's always been and how he always will be, I reckon. Why didn't you even tell the poor girl 'bout that? If I was almost a state champion in football I would wear it like a badge! Hell, I'd told everybody even if I just met 'em. Joe Baird, almost a state champion, know what I mean? Hell, I'd be proud of it! No, but it isn't like John Boy to be proud of anything. No, he'd like to think of himself as born to no one. He'd rather he just fell out of the sky, I reckon. Ain't that right, John? You'd like to just disassociate yourself from your family like you're really something. Ain't that right, John Boy? You don't want to tell her you're a Baird. Almost a state champion. Nah, you don't want to tell her that. You're a man with no past... like Charles Bronson. Ain't that right, John Boy? Only come when you want to...

JOHN BOY: I brought her here, didn't I?

JOE: Yes, you did. You did that much. That much is true... He brought you here. That's a step in the right direction, I suppose. First girl he's ever brought around here. Why is that, John Boy? Why is she the first girl you've ever brought around here? I know you ain't queer. I seen the pictures you got laying around the house.

JOHN BOY: I don't do that anymore.

JOE: He used to have the pictures laying around the house. Can you believe it? The dirty kind. Hustler. I am a man but I mean, I'd never touch that sort of filth. Too dirty. Of course, not for John Boy. He likes that kind of filth. He must to have it all over the house, girls in all kinds of strange positions... showing their... you know, particulars. Incredible to think it now. I brought him up to be that way... strong, tough, and liking women. Turned out alright... mostly.

ROSE: It's a real pleasure to meet you, Mr. Baird. It really is.

JOE: Why thank you, little girlie. Call me Joe. That's what everybody calls me around here.

ROSE: Okay, Joe.

JOE: And the pleasure is... all mine, really. You are really well built. Anybody ever told you that, that you're well built?

ROSE: Yes...

JOE: Oh, I guess it's a usual thing?

ROSE: No. Not really usual. Not all the time. I'm from a small town.

JOE: So if you were from a big city you'd probably expect to hear it more often. Is that it?

Rose smiles uncomfortably.

JOE: Mercy!

JOHN BOY: Okay, Pop! For God sakes, she knows. Shut up already!

JOE: You watch your mouth. I'm just making conversation. I suppose you'd like to sit here and say nothing. Is that it, John Boy? I'm sorry, Rose. I never quite taught him discipline. He wouldn't have any of it. He was going to do what he wanted to do when he wanted to do it and there wasn't nothing anybody could do to stop it.

Rose smiles uncomfortably.

JOE: But like I was saying, you are a beautiful girl. I'm surprised you'd be interested in the boy, but that's your choice. *Suddenly interested.* WHY are you interested?

ROSE: Well, John is the nicest man I think I ever met. *She looks at John.* And the most handsome...

JOE: *Pause.* Don't get out much, do you? Where did you say you were from?

ROSE: Lampasas.

JOE: Well, what were you doing in Amarillo?

ROSE: I was waiting for a bus to New Mexico to see family.

JOHN BOY: She don't have to tell you all that!

JOE: I'm just making conversation, John Boy. Just trying to get better acquainted with the young lady, that's all.

JOHN BOY: Don't be getting acquainted too much! Don't be getting too personal!

JOE: Why? What's the trouble with getting personal? We're all family here. Aren't we... Honey Rose?

ROSE: We will be.

JOHN BOY: And her name is not Honey Rose. It's Rose. Just Rose.

JOE: God bless you, darlin', for wanting to put up with my boy. I know he's hard to handle. But they say there's a "perfect fit" out there for everybody, no matter how stubborn and hot-headed the person may be.

JOHN BOY: Drink up that lemonade, Rose. We're going soon.

JOE: What's wrong, John Boy? You just got here. What are you in such a rush for to leave? I'm enjoyin' the company. Rose is enjoying the company. Aren't you, Rose?

ROSE: Yes, sir.

JOE: Call me Daddy. See there. She's been reared good calling me sir. Must come from a good family. Taught her manners. *Thinking.* Shit. Did I leave the stove on? Hold on.

He walks away for a moment.

ROSE: Is everything okay, John? If you don't want to be here, we can go.

JOHN BOY: I don't care. He's always acting normal anytime I bring somebody over. He's always done that. Don't get conned into thinking he's a nice guy! He ain't!

ROSE: Oh, he doesn't seem like he means any harm.

She combs his hair out of his face.

ROSE: I just thought it'd be nice to meet your family. I know it means a lot to him you coming down here and visiting like this.

JOHN BOY: Okay. But well, you don't have to take him staring you up and down like he is.

ROSE: He's just an old man, sweetheart. They all do that.

JOHN BOY: I know he's gonna look but he can look at someone else. I wanna be the only one looking at you like that.

ROSE: We're doing the right thing, John. You'll see... you never know what you got until it's gone.

JOHN BOY: Yeah, I know.

Rose looks far off as if she is thinking about someone else who is no longer with us.

JOE: How's the heat in here? You both warm enough? I'll throw another log in the furnace if you'd like.

ROSE: I'm okay.

JOE: Just as good. Boy, it's been a cold winter. You okay, John Boy?

JOHN BOY: Yeah, Pop.

JOE: John Boy gets cold easily. You'll know his mother had to put ten blankets on him as a child just to warm him up!

JOHN BOY: That's not true.

JOE: Well, it was a lot. Boy, he was very particular about that. He likes that warm weather. He can't get enough of it. Some of them boys like to work in offices! Not my John Boy. He's a working man. He likes to feel that hot sun beating down on him. If he ain't sweating it ain't work for him. That's how the Bairds are, have always been. We come from a long line of strong hard-working genes. It's a good gene pool, that's for sure! *Short pause.* You looking to have a baby with my boy?

ROSE: I—

JOHN BOY: Hey! What'd I tell you about that?

JOE: What?

JOHN BOY: We barely got the ball rolling on this marriage thing. We're gonna get hitched! You don't need to be asking all them crazy questions!

ROSE: It's okay, John.

JOE: Well, I'm interested! *Said like "intrsted" with no vowels.* Can't your old man be a little interested in the Baird name? How do you think I feel popping out two boys who won't have kids? Time's running out on me, boy! It's not right for an old man like myself to not have grandchildren! It's not natural!

JOHN BOY: Alright, alright.

JOE, *continuing:* At first I thought your brother was just a fluke. Bad seed. Then you come along and read your magazines and throw away that good seed like there's no tomorrow! Can't you see you gotta do something with it, otherwise it's gone. Gone forever! Wasted... with all that potential! Youth sure is wasted on the wrong people.

JOHN BOY: Yeah, yeah, alright. Don't you know what unpleasant conversation is?

JOE: I'm sorry, but right or wrong I've been thinking... about all the Bairds that have come before me. Look at your cousins. Your poor, poor cousins. You really think that's the best us Bairds can do? *Pause.* Hell no! You've got responsibility, boy, to pop out something better! And I suspect that this here little lady is just brimmin' with potential. Yes sir, this is fertile soil, indeed.

JOHN BOY: Stop it.

JOE: You better get going with that girl and never leave her for a second! If she gets out enough she's liable to see what she's missing and the mistake she's made going off with a schlub like you!

JOHN BOY: That's it! I've had it.

JOE: What? What'd I say?

JOHN BOY: You said enough, Pop. I've done my duty. I paid my respects. We're gettin' married and that's it. I'll send you the pictures.

JOE, *matter-of-factly:* Okay. I'll put 'em up. Frame 'em real nice and put 'em up.

JOHN BOY: I don't care what you do with them. They'll be yours to keep.

John Boy grabs Rose and heads for the door.

JOE: Alright, John Boy. Thanks for dropping by. You know you and your wife are always welcome.

ROSE: Thank you.

JOHN BOY, *unimpressed:* Yeah...

JOE: Okay, son. You remember what I said.

JOHN BOY: How can I forget the things you say, Pop?

JOE: You know, about the kids… don't rush it, but if you're having problems, keep on trying. We're behind in the count, if you know what I mean.

John Boy rolls his eyes.

JOHN BOY: Yeah, whatever.

JOE: Can I get one more hug from my new daughter-in-law? *He smiles devilishly as Rose obliges.* We're just one big happy family. You remember that. Okay, son. Call me if you need anything.

John Boy looks at him incredulously.

JOHN BOY: What's your deal, Pop?

JOE: What do you mean?

JOHN BOY: Why you actin' like you care all of a sudden?

JOE, *short pause:* I'm sorry if I treated you like a jackass all these years, son. My fault. My fault if we got started off on the wrong foot… Of course, I care. You're my son, my own flesh and blood.

John Boy is taken aback by this. He doesn't know quite what to say.

JOHN BOY, *short pause:* Weird...

John Boy grabs Rose's hand and walks out. Rose waves at Joe, who waves back with a shit-eating grin on his face.

JOE: Be careful on the road, son. God forbid you hit a pothole and make the poor girl infertile! And remember to wear the boxers, not the briefs!

Joe watches as John Boy gets into his car. The sound of John Boy's car peeling out. Joe locks the door, walks back to the recliner, and picks up where he left off shining his shotgun.

LIGHTS OUT

THE HOMELESS SECRETARY

Gerry Sheridan

THE HOMELESS SECRETARY was originally performed at the Producer's Club in New York City. Directed by Brian Chicocki

STARRING

Denise Lute as Pat
Todd Reichart as Joe
Victor Hawks as Nick

PLACE:

Office, New York City

TIME:

The Present

Scene opens when Pat runs in carrying her coat. She throws it down and starts typing at the computer while simultaneously kicking off sneakers and putting on shoes.

PAT: Come on, come on print! Shit, shit, shit!

Puts on shoes and then looks back at the computer.

PAT, *to computer:* Yes, I'm sure!

Pat runs offstage to get papers out of printer. Joe walks in eating a donut the same moment Pat runs in with papers.

JOE: Oh, you're here.

PAT: Yeah. Here are your e-mails.

JOE: Thanks. Did you send that invoice yet?

PAT: Ah, I'm working on it now.

Joe starts to leave.

JOE: Oh, this came for you today. *Joe pulls paper out of jacket.* Sorry, I didn't mean to take it. I mean, the guy said "Pat Patterson?" And I said yes. And before I could finish and say, "Yes, she works here," he said "you've been served" and shoved it in my hand and walked away. I didn't mean to pry or anything. If you need to talk I'm always available.

Pat opens the envelope.

PAT: You're eating a donut? Don't you have a cholesterol test tomorrow?

JOE: Oh yeah, I forgot.

PAT: Those things are full of fat, they're like fried. Eeeew...

JOE: Ah... you're right. Nuts.

He throws it in the wastebasket. Joe goes offstage. Pat reaches into the wastebasket and takes out the donut, eating it ravenously. She dials the phone.

PAT: Hello? Hello is this Mrs. Mathews? Hi, yeah, this is Pat Patterson. Patricia, yeah. Yes, that's what I'm calling about. You know, I really think you should give me a break this one time. I can't believe one transgression and I'm like cut off. Someone once said, "The quality of mercy is not strained," – well I think it is at American Express. Isn't a person allowed to make a mistake? Can't you give me a little more time?

Look, what happened was, I wrote a check for three thousand dollars to American Express, but I put it in the wrong envelope and mailed it to Sprint instead. Then I went online to order a new ID tag for my dog, and somehow I got my zip code in the little box that says how many tags you want, so instead of ordering one, I accidentally ordered eleven thousand two hundred and one. That's my zip code, 11201. And I used my debit card so it completely wiped out my account so now even though I want to, I can't send you a check for three thousand dollars until the dispute is settled. Doesn't anyone even look at these things? Couldn't someone have said, "Gee, this looks a little funny, who would need eleven thousand two hundred and one gold toned dog tags with the name Mitzi on them and the same address? Can you believe it? I hit confirm and my entire life is in a shambles? At $2.95 a piece those tags cost over thirty-three thousand dollars plus shipping and handling.

So, I have every intention of paying you and I think that should count for something. I'll get paid a week from Tuesday and I can send you something then. I even had to stop my company from doing direct deposit because I was afraid every penny was going to be sucked up by that stupid dog tag company.

JOE, *from offstage*: Pat!

PAT: Oh my god. Listen, can you hold on a minute? Please, please, PLEASE? I'll be right back, I swear. *Pat puts the phone on hold.*

Joe enters.

JOE: Pat, are you sure this is right? This sounds weird. Crispy clumps, crunchy clumps, and light and airy clumps?

Joe shows her the document.

PAT, *talking fast:* Yeah, that's right. Crispy clumps, crunchy clumps, light and airy clumps.

JOE: Are you sure?

PAT: Yeah, look, it's on page seventeen of the original document. Here it is; crispy clumps, crunchy clumps, and light and airy clumps.

JOE: I don't know if "clumps" sounds appetizing. Are people gonna wanna buy a clumpy breakfast cereal?

PAT: This research cost seventy-five thousand dollars. I'm sure they know what they're doing.

JOE: Ok, yeah, I guess. You're a smart cookie, Patty.

Joe goes offstage. Pat picks up phone.

PAT: Mrs. Mathews? Oh, I'm so sorry. Thanks for waiting. You know, I think when the moon goes out of its present void state that things will get better. I don't even have my ATM card right now because I accidentally left it in this cosmetics store I just had to go into because they have products from all over the world. Douglas

Cosmetics. I got some really good bath products there. You should try it.

So, Mrs. Mathews, please don't cut me off. Think about it. I make one mistake and immediately the trappings of civilization start to fall away. My cell phone is turned off. I have no credit card. My gym membership is on hold because they charge my credit card. And I have no money for food. So if you don't help me out I will starve to death, Mrs. Mathews.

I am, I am on a total economy kick now, so I will get caught up. This was really weird – someone gave me this book on Zen and I opened it at random and read "Life is suffering. Suffering is caused by selfish craving. Selfish craving can be overcome!" It was like some sort of message for me and I knew right then that I could stop shopping and I haven't bought a thing. I have bought nothing at all, it's amazing. *Listens.* Well, I haven't bought anything since Saturday anyway, that's pretty good.

So, please, Mrs. Mathews, think about the human side to all these numbers you see, you know? There must be a way, some way to keep my card afloat, huh? Mrs. Mathews? Hello? Hello? Mrs. Mathews? Hello? Oh my god, she hung up! Fuck, fuck, fucker!

Joe comes back out.

JOE: I'm still thinking about the clumps.

PAT: Ah, Joe, I need to talk to you about something.

JOE: This is important. It's not right. What's the box gonna say? Now with light and airy clumps? This is bad. It could bring the whole company down.

PAT: Would you forget about the clumps for a minute!

JOE: We can't turn out this kind of work. We're going down.

PAT: It doesn't matter. Believe me. Would you listen?

JOE: We're gonna have to start over. I'm gonna pull the plug on the whole thing.

PAT: Joe, I need to talk to you. Remember you said if I ever needed to talk you'd be there. Remember?

JOE: Yeah, but this is serious. If the client doesn't like it, my job is on the line. I have a family and now the kid wants a horse. Can you believe that? A horse! I tried to tell him we don't come from horse people. He doesn't care. The clumps aren't gonna go away unless we do something.

PAT: Joe, stop – listen, there's a human being in front of you that needs help and you're talking about clumps. Remember that donut you threw in the wastebasket?

JOE: Yeah.

PAT: I ate it.

JOE: Oh my god.

PAT: I also walked to work.

JOE: Uh-huh.

PAT: And I live in Brooklyn. I'm in a terrible mess. Would you focus and listen to me now?

JOE: Okay. Shoot.

PAT: This is what came today – pry, pry away.

JOE: You're being evicted?

PAT: Yeah, and I have no money and if I don't get an advance I'm gonna starve and end up homeless. Can I get an advance on my paycheck?

JOE: Ah, well, I guess we could get the paperwork to accounting and see.

PAT: How long would it take?

JOE: They usually take a couple of weeks.

PAT: A couple of weeks? How is it an advance if it comes after my paycheck? Forget that – how about a bonus? Can I get a bonus?

JOE: That'll be tough – it's not in this year's budget.

PAT: Why don't you just put in a few more of these?

Holds up paper.

JOE: What's that?

PAT: Your expense report. You put in four things that you charged on the company credit card so they're like paying for it twice.

JOE: Is this blackmail?

PAT: It's a barometer of the amount of desperation I feel.

JOE: I never look at those receipts. I figured if something was going in twice you'd catch it. That's why I give them to you.

PAT: Oh my god. I'm so sorry. I'm sorry. Crap.

JOE: Don't you have any family that can help you?

PAT: No.

JOE: Really.

PAT: Yeah, it's just the way it is. It's no biggie. Did you see the article in the Times about all the elderly people there are now who have no one to call in case of emergency?

JOE: Yeah.

PAT: Well, me and the octogenarians are in the same boat.

JOE: What happened? Why are you in trouble?

PAT: Internet shopping mishap...

Joe looks at computer.

PAT: It wasn't during work!

JOE: Well, I used to shop. Until I found myself buying back the same Rolexes I had sold for twice the price. Then I figured it was time to move on to something else. So instead of shopping, I run. You should try it.

PAT: I will. I will, I swear. I promise to jog my way to financial freedom when this is over, but right now I need money.

Joe takes a post-it off Pat's desk and writes down church info.

JOE: What also helped me is Reverend Jimmy and his Church Against Shopping. It's really interesting. He says consumerism is a totalizing system and a secretly administered trance state and that we need to magicalize our experience.

Joe hands her the post-it.

PAT: Yeah? Maybe that's why up till now my idea of a good investment was an expensive winter coat.

JOE: I would've joined his group, but I work in marketing.

PAT: Ok, yeah, um, I'll look him up as soon as I know I'm not gonna be homeless. You know, this whole city is full of assistants and secretaries on the brink of homelessness. I swear it's not just me. We have no cushion.

JOE: Ah, I don't know what to tell you.

PAT: Joe, please!

Enter Nick, More-Tags Representative.

NICK: Excuse me, is one of you Pat Patterson?

PAT: Yeah, ah, that's me.

NICK: Oh, how do you do? I'm Nick DeSantis from More Tags.

PAT: What? What are you doing here? You've hunted me down at my office? I don't believe this!

NICK: I understand there is a dispute with my company and I wanted to ask you a few questions.

JOE: Maybe I should go.

PAT: No, no, we never get a chance to talk and we're not finished. Don't go!

NICK: Please rate on a scale of one to ten your satisfaction with ease of use at Moretags.com.

PAT: Uh, ah – two. Joe, please. There must be a way.

JOE: I wish there was.

NICK: Would you recommend More Tags to a friend?

PAT: No. How many years have I worked for you and never asked you for anything?

JOE: A long time.

NICK: On a scale of one to five please rate your overall experience with Moretags.com.

PAT: Overall? Um, let me see… can we say, "You ruined my life, you bastards?"

NICK: I'll write a one.

JOE: Ah, I'm sorry, I got things to do.

PAT: Wait!

NICK: If you had not purchased these items from Moretags, where would you have purchased them? Petco, Petcare, Petsmart, Petstreet, Petcenter, Yourpet or a local pet store?

JOE: This is so boring, I don't know how I'm standing up.

PAT: Joe, please…

JOE: Look, I really have to get back to my desk.

NICK: Ah, excuse me, did you hear the question or should I repeat it? You know Petsmart, Petco, Petcare…

PAT: Petstore! Petstore! Joe wait!

NICK: Ok, good.

JOE: I have to get to work on the clump problem.

PAT: Joe, why is this such a big deal? Any fool could come up with viable alternatives to clumps!

JOE: Yeah? What? *Pause.*

PAT: I know, but I'm not telling.

JOE: What?

NICK: In the past three months have you used the Internet to browse or research products before making a purchase?

PAT: Yes. No more freebies. What's in all this for me?

JOE: Patty?

PAT: It's gonna cost ya.

NICK: When performing web research do you prefer a particular search engine? For example, Google, Yahoo, MSN, AOL, My Way, Ask Jeeves?

PAT: Research? Ah yeah, Google. Research, yeah. Ok, here's the deal. I redo the entire market research document with new results and you pay me two-thirds of what you would've paid them.

JOE: You think you'd be able to?

PAT: Definitely. *Pause.* I can even pull together some focus groups on twenty-four hour notice. I have a bunch of actor friends and if you offer them fifty dollars they'll show up with like two-hour notice. And they all have college degrees so it makes for a very upscale low-scale group.

JOE: I don't know.

NICK: Did you find Moretags as a result of one of these searches?

JOE: You really think you can do this?

PAT: Yes. I swear I can. I'll incorporate today so you can make the check out to Mitzi Productions.

JOE: Just don't go near flakes. They'll lose credibility if they go anywhere near flakes.

PAT: I promise. I promise.

JOE: Okay, deal. Two-thirds. *They shake hands.*

PAT: A preview; huddles, bunches, clusters, gatherings, hordes, bouquets, gangs, jamborees....

NICK: Nuggets.

PAT: See, we're not stuck!

JOE: Impressive!

PAT: English degree.

JOE: Okay. Here's the report. Just don't let me down. Hey, we figured something out. You see, there's nothing in the budget for human problems, per se. But this is good.

NICK, *to Joe:* Would you like a subscription to Dog Fancy?

JOE: Can I leave now?

PAT: Yes. Thank you. Thank you. *Joe exits.* Two-thirds of seventy-five thousand! Ah... um... Oh my god, that's fifty thousand dollars! Thank you! Thank you! I can't believe it! Something good just happened. I never thought anything good was actually gonna happen in my life! Do you believe it? I can't believe it!

Pat hugs Nick.

NICK: I'm happy for you.

PAT: I could even afford to buy the dog tags now.

NICK: Great.

PAT: But I'm not gonna.

NICK: Oh.

PAT: But if I did I could make like a huge like art installation sculpture of a giant dog made out of eleven thousand two hundred and one gold toned dog tags and I could call it Mitzi.

NICK: Mitzi.

PAT: But it would be an impulse buy and I'm done with impulse shopping. The only thing I'm buying for the next year is a jogging suit. Do you realize that I've been in a trance state when I bought anything?

NICK: Oh wow, that's heavy.

PAT: I know, right?

NICK: Maybe that explains why in one week I bought three DVD burners off of the EBay.

PAT: How did that work out?

NICK: Luckily, I know a good repairman.

PAT: See!

NICK: And I had to hide them in the closet so my wife wouldn't know.

PAT: Trance! Trance! Maybe it's a government plot or something. Maybe if people like us save money it isn't good for the economy.

NICK: Man, I don't know. Ah...

Looks at clipboard.

PAT: Just fill in the rest the way you think I would answer. I have work to do. Do you have to do this all day?

NICK: Believe me, sometimes I even give myself a headache. Bye, Miss Patterson.

PAT: Bye.

Nick starts to leave.

NICK: Oh, I forgot, I have to do one thing. *Reads.* We at Moretags hope we can reach a successful resolution to the ongoing dispute relating to your purchase. To show good faith, we would like to give you this gift certificate for two dollars and fifty cents towards your next purchase at Moretags. Thank you.

Nick leaves and Pat starts looking through the document and typing at the computer. She picks up the gift certificate and looks at it for a moment, then throws it in the waste basket and goes back to work.

BLACKOUT

DAWNLESS DAYS

Olivia Arieti

DAWNLESS DAYS has had a staged reading by the Baywrite Theatre Group in Byron Bay, Australia.

CHARACTERS

MEG: *In her thirties. An Outback girl.*

JEFF: *In his thirties. A Welsh miner.*

DEAN: *In his twenties. A truck driver.*

SETTING:

A bed-sit in an Outback mining town.

TIME:

Evening. Next morning.

SCENE 1

At rise, MEG and DEAN are on the threshold. Dean is leaving. He is kissing her passionately.

DEAN: I'll be back soon, sweetheart... within a few weeks I'll be holding you in my arms again.

MEG: You have to go now, darling, it's late...

DEAN: I know, Meg, just one last kiss... it's been lovely... I'd go on forever. *Kisses her again.* I want you to find a solution, honey... the sooner the better.

MEG, *uneasy:* I will, but you really must go... Don't want him to find you here.

DEAN: Don't worry, I'm leaving... You'll tell him, baby, won't you?

MEG: I'm afraid he already knows.

DEAN: You'll talk to him clearly this time...

MEG: I'll do it...

DEAN: Promise?

MEG, *nods:* Promise.

DEAN: So long, dear, take care.

MEG: Bye, Dean.

Dean exits. Truck engine fades in distance. Meg brushes her hair. Turns on the radio. Starts preparing supper. JEFF enters back from the mine very shabby and tired.

JEFF, *hangs up his waistcoat:* Hi, Meg. Home at last, really feel exhausted. *Wipes his sweat.* This heat is unbearable. Don't know how long I'll be able to stand it. It paralyzes all my functions.

MEG: It does.

JEFF: What do you mean?

MEG: You understood perfectly, Jeff.

JEFF, *gets a beer:* You can't pretend a Welsh to find himself at ease in this desert. Miles and miles of dry red land under a blazing dry red sun. Whatever can come out of it?

MEG: My family has always lived here… for generations.

JEFF, *moves close to her:* You are an exception: a rare opal with a fresh cut.

MEG, *steps back, disgusted:* You stopped at Chuck's, I bet.

JEFF: Just a sip to kill the heat. *Coughs.* You know how dusty even throats get down here. *Opens the fridge.* Hey, better put some more beers in the fridge.

MEG: Sure, they're never enough for you.

JEFF: Can't you turn off that radio, for heaven's sake? I've still got the air hammer in my ears. Don't know how, but it always gets through. *Opens the cupboard.* Oh, he's been here, I see.

MEG: Just left the necessary things.

JEFF: Only that?

MEG: What do you mean?

JEFF, *puts the beers in the fridge:* You understood perfectly.

MEG: Dinner is almost ready. Are you going to wash up?

JEFF: No, I'm too tired. Have to take me as I am, my dear. *Pause, ironically.* Say, you sure have a lot of men around you for being in this forlorn little square of earth.

Sits down.

MEG: If I hadn't visited my ex-husband you wouldn't have met me.

JEFF: Never understood the necessity of going on seeing him.

MEG, *serves the dinner:* He's my ex-husband after all. We're still friends. *Sits down.* Poor Harry... he misses me, I know it. Just couldn't keep up with the life down here in the Outback.

JEFF: You bet.

MEG: He wanted to take me with him.

JEFF: Why didn't you go? You sound nostalgic.

MEG: I couldn't. I was part of the Outback, not of him.

JEFF: Are you part of me?

MEG: It's not an easy question. You don't belong here.

JEFF: I know. Perhaps, it's this heat's fault.

MEG: The heat's?

JEFF: Yeah, I constantly think of home… in Wales, with its green hills, its bitter sea breeze hitting the cliffs… sort of feel homesick, probably an outcast too.

MEG: It's difficult to get used to this place. A foreigner always ends up wishing to go back where he comes from. Quite normal...

JEFF: Do all newcomers go on being strangers forever?

MEG: Most do.

JEFF, *moves close:* Listen, honey... *Takes her hand...* Couldn't we try again?

MEG: It's useless, Jeff. *Withdraws her hand.* We did… so many times and it never worked out. No point going on being disappointed.

JEFF: You can't be so definite!

MEG: Probably if we didn't lose the baby…

JEFF: I suffered a lot too, Meg, believe me.

MEG: The situation would have been different.

JEFF: It might happen again, darling, we are still young, there could be a whole life ahead of us… *Holds her in his arms.* Meg, dear, I still care for you… a lot… give us another chance.

MEG, *frees herself:* I can't. It's too late.

JEFF: Why?! Because of Dean? You can't have fallen head over heels for him!

MEG: He will be coming back soon. *Pause.* We must talk about it.

JEFF: Do you want me to leave?

MEG: I'm confused, don't know what's best for me, for us.

JEFF: He runs from one place to the other and never stops for more than a night.

MEG: You are implying what you shouldn't. Are you jealous?

JEFF: Should I?

MEG: He belongs to this land, always done this job, like his father and grandfathers. His truck runs miles and miles everyday, knows every inch of it.

JEFF: Does he know every inch of you?

MEG: You're a bloody bastard, Jeff.

JEFF, *shouts:* What shall I do? Pack up and leave? Or stay here and watch you crave for a man who every week or two stops in a house where a lonely woman has nothing better to do than wait and fancy over some possible exciting encounter?

MEG: You'll never understand our way.

JEFF, *gets another beer:* I understand his, baby.

MEG, *angry:* How dare you denigrate his work?

JEFF: I'm denigrating his feelings, nothing else.

MEG: What about yours?

JEFF: I told you about mine.

MEG: Let's face it, Jeff, it's over. We tried over and over again but now we're through.

JEFF: I can't stand your determination. *Pause.* You liked it once, however.

MEG: Yeah, I was happy at the beginning, sort of felt comfortable with you. Thought you would make it, but you didn't. That's it.

JEFF: Can't put all the blame on me. Working in the mine kills you.

MEG: What did you expect?

JEFF: As soon as you get out, happy to find yourself in the sunlight again, you are immediately overwhelmed by this damned heat. Breathing becomes as hard as working.

MEG: It's because it isn't your place. Our desert can turn into a trap if you aren't part of it. It's a land of extremes, harsh and unforgiving... nothing to do with yours.

JEFF: Like you?

MEG: It's not my fault if our life together has turned out so miserable.

JEFF, *moves close to her:* I know things haven't been going too well lately... but please, Meg, consider the possibility of staying with me... We could get out of here, I might find another job by the coast, where we can settle down, get married... Let's try again, honey, I'm sure I'll be able to make you happy, trust me.

MEG: I've already trusted you and what did you do? Got sloppier and sloppier and ended up drinking.

JEFF: I'll give that up, as long as you stay with me... I promise. The situation sort of slipped out of my hands... didn't realise how low I was falling.

MEG: You never considered what I really wanted, what I needed.

JEFF: You didn't do much either except listening to that stupid radio.

MEG: I wanted to complete my education.

JEFF: Or looking out of that damned window!

MEG: Nothing else to do, my dear, you spent all our money left on alcohol.

JEFF: Never even made up the bed.

MEG: Didn't think it necessary. You were too drunk to use it.

JEFF: Did you obsess your ex-husband like that?

MEG: It's none of your business.

JEFF, *gets hold of her:* Listen, baby, it's my business alright! We're here together, nearly had a child, everyday I break my back for you and I won't let you walk out with some lousy tough guy you just met!

MEG, *tries to free herself:* Let me go, Jeff, you're hurting me. You're drunk as usual.

JEFF, *holds her tighter:* I won't let you go, Meg. And I'm not drunk at all.

MEG, *frightened:* Jeff, please!

JEFF: Let me kiss you, baby, there might be nothing else in this damned desert except heat, locusts, and fucking dust, but you are my woman and I am your man. I want you, Meg, and I'm going to have you.

Throws her on the bed. Black Out.

SCENE 2

At rise the next morning, Meg is preparing breakfast. Jeff enters shaved and neat.

JEFF: Just heard the news... the dust storm will be here any minute. Better start shutting the windows.

MEG: There is still time. Warnings are always quite in advance. *Smiles.* You look fine this morning, Jeff, even shaved...

JEFF: Had to change somehow... *Moves close to her uneasily.* I'm sorry, Meg, I really shouldn't have forced you into it.

MEG: One night's excitement can't wipe out the shallowness of all the others.

JEFF: I know. The fact is that you are too attractive, honey.

MEG, *smiles:* Well, I must admit you made me feel so.

JEFF, *looks at her:* So beautiful... especially in the morning.

MEG: Perhaps we—

JEFF: No, you don't have to say anything... the fault is mine. I... I sort of lost my head last night... Besides, the idea of losing you was so unbearable... I've thought things over...

MEG: So did I...

JEFF: I was so upset, I couldn't sleep.

MEG, *smiles:* I felt exhausted but slept quite well.

JEFF: Of course, I realise I haven't been behaving properly lately...
I'm really sorry, Meg.

MEG: So you are?

JEFF: Last night was different though... admit it, honey.

Moves closer.

MEG: Coffee is ready.

Serves the coffee.

JEFF: You liked it.

MEG: I did, it was like the first time.

JEFF, *happy:* I was sure about it. *Sits down.* I agree that one night
can't change everything... but if we—

*Sound of truck engine. Meg runs to the window. Jack looks at her.
Shakes his head.*

MEG, *turns round:* What were you saying?

JEFF, *drinks his coffee:* Bah. Never mind.

Wind howls.

MEG: Listen, Jeff—

JEFF, *angry:* It's useless looking out, that wasn't his truck! He won't
be coming for quite a while, love.

MEG: I know... I wasn't thinking of him.

JEFF: Oh, you weren't? I'm sure you were, instead.

MEG: You'll never stop being so stupidly jealous.

JEFF: Hope this damned storm gets over. The sooner, the better... for both of us.

MEG: All these months I felt as if our days had become dawnless, dull and grey as sandstorms. Ones, with no more future, but strangely something has —

JEFF, *shouts:* Sure, no past, no present, no future! Where do you think your future is? Here? Waiting for a man who'll show up once in a while?

MEG: Leave him out of this, Jeff. You know nothing about him.

JEFF, *moves close to her:* I know about you, my dear. I realise you aren't able to love at all, this heat has dried out all your feelings too.

MEG: Your drinking has soaked yours instead.

JEFF, *shakes his head:* I've been foolish to believe we might have had another chance. Sorry if I insisted.

MEG: You never understand, Jeff.

JEFF, *grabs her arm:* Admit it, Meg, you don't know what you really want, what you're looking for. Yours is a desperate search for water, but nothing can really quench your thirst.

MEG, *shouts:* You want to put all the blame on me, that's what you want!

JEFF: I'm aware of my faults and tried to make up for them.

MEG: Did you believe it would be so easy? Do you know how many nights I cried myself to sleep?

JEFF, *ironic:* Are you able to cry? Never knew it.

MEG: It rains here too, and it rains a lot.

JEFF: It's too late when it rains, I'm afraid, the land is too dry to let the water in, just like your heart.

MEG: Why didn't you stay where you belonged? It would have been better for both.

JEFF: I believe you're right. Probably you understood it long before I did. Or perhaps I did too, simply didn't want to accept it. *Starts taking things out of drawers.* It wasn't the heat or the work in the mine. It was you.

MEG: What are you doing?

JEFF: I'm getting things ready. *Takes out a suitcase.* I'm going back home.

MEG, *surprised:* To Wales?

JEFF, *puts his clothes in it:* No use going anywhere else... I'm tired, exhausted... always felt homesick so I might as well go back there.

MEG: A sudden decision...

JEFF: I suppose it is. Definite, however.

MEG: Thought you didn't want to go.

JEFF: So did I... but now I believe this is the best thing for me to do and you'll do what's best for you. I feel like changing, hoped I could have done it with you, but since this is not possible, I'll do it on my own.

MEG: Are you convinced?

JEFF: Too much work, too much drinking… too much hassle. I need some rest.

MEG, *defiantly:* I might be pregnant.

JEFF, *a moment of hesitation:* Is there a chance I might be the father?

MEG: You make me pray I'm not!

JEFF: Let me know if I am the lucky guy. *Hesitates.* If you want to, of course...

MEG, *looks out of the window:* How long will the storm last?

JEFF: Long enough for me to get ready and for you to get used to the idea.

BLACKOUT
THE END

A GOOD KID

Bill Mesce Jr.

A GOOD KID has received a number of productions in New Jersey and New York, won for Best Play and Audience Favorite at the Turnip Theatre One-Act Festival in New York, and was a semi-finalist in the Annual Off-Off Broadway Original Short Play Festival, also in New York. The piece led to several "sequels" which were also produced in the area and eventually combined into the full-length A JERSEY CANTATA which also won or was in the running for several awards.

SETTING: *A funeral home*

SCENE 1

A funeral home. At rise, BILLY BONES sits in a row of chairs. On a table next to him is a small metal strong box and a small ledger. A lit votive. Candle sits on the table near a headshot photograph of a young man. Enter JOHN.

JOHN: Yo! Who's that? Yo, Billy Bones!

BILLY, *rising:* Hey, John! *A warm handshake.* How's it goin', Big John?

JOHN: Ah, how *you* doin'?

BILLY: I'm doin'.

JOHN: Everything's all right?

BILLY, *nodding offstage:* Well, you know, all things considered...

JOHN: Well, yeah. Your mother? How's she doin'?

BILLY: Fine. She was by before. She asked.

JOHN: Well, she's a peach. *A sad look offstage.* You believe this?

BILLY, *shrugging:* Hey.

John signs the ledger by the box, then sticks some cash into the box.

JOHN: I mean, hey, what a shame, ya know?

BILLY: I know.

JOHN: But you're doin' ok?

BILLY: Gettin' by.

JOHN: You still over at Eddie Bear's?

BILLY: Still.

JOHN: That's good.

BILLY: It's all right.

JOHN: I mean things goin' ok over there?

BILLY: The usual, you know?

JOHN: Eddie's a good guy.

BILLY: Yeah, he is.

JOHN: Jesus, when was the last time?

BILLY: It's been a while, John. You don't come around.

JOHN: Not enough hours in the day, know what I'm sayin'?

BILLY: You don't have to tell me.

JOHN: Jesus, I haven't seen my old lady in what? Six months? That's my mother, it's six months.

BILLY: Long time.

JOHN: Yeah, long time. Too long, you're right. Some things, you got to make the time, right?

BILLY: Got to make the time, John.

JOHN: Yeah, well…

BILLY: Wind up seein' people, it's always weddings and funerals.

JOHN: Christenings. Get 'em comin' and goin'.

BILLY: Hey, you're busy, what're you gonna do?

JOHN: I should make the time, I know. Shouldn't wait for, well...

BILLY: Yeah.

JOHN: Hey, what're you doin' back here? You watchin' the box?

BILLY: I told 'em I'd watch the box for a while. You know. Give 'em a break.

JOHN: Billy Bones, watchin' the box. That's like lettin' Capone guard the mint.

BILLY, *admonishing:* Hey, John.

JOHN: Sorry, sorry. Not here, you're right, you're right. Hey, you mind if I sit with you? I, uh, I don't want to go back in there right now.

BILLY: Yeah, sure. Sit.

JOHN: I need a break, you know?

BILLY: Yeah.

JOHN: It's hard enough, right? Then you see her there, his mother, all like that...

BILLY: It's tough, you don't have to tell me. Sit.

They sit. John fumbles out a cigarette then stops himself.

JOHN: I just need a break. Hey, can I smoke here?

BILLY: They got a room downstairs. I don't think up here.

JOHN: Ah, screw 'em.

John starts to light cigarette with the candle but a reprimanding look from Billy stops him. John shrugs apologetically and puts the cigarette away.

JOHN: So, how you been?

BILLY: Ah, you know, like I said. Okay. I could've done without hearing this.

JOHN: Hey, you and me both, brother. Right? Jeez, I just saw him… When was it? I dunno, it wasn't that long…What's this, April? Oh, well, hey, it was a coupla months ago. But he looked fine. I mean, you know, not great or anything. He never looked great.

BILLY: That's true.

JOHN: I mean, I know he wasn't, he was, you know, I knew he was sick, but he looked fine. I mean, he didn't look like, you know…

BILLY: Well, like you said, that was a coupla months ago.

JOHN: I didn't think, you know, like that was fast.

BILLY: I guess. There's no schedule.

JOHN: Yeah, I know. It just seemed fast. Maybe I should've come around. I just didn't think it'd be that fast. It doesn't feel that long ago I saw him and he looked okay.

BILLY: I remember when my old man went…you remember?

JOHN: Hey, he was what? A year and a half sick? Almost two years?

BILLY: What two years? You go from the first heart attack, it's like four years. Four years from the first heart attack.

JOHN: But he was okay after that, after that first time.

BILLY: What okay?

JOHN: I mean he was alright.

BILLY: What alright? He was gettin' around, yeah, but he wasn't workin' or nothin'. He was on disability and he had to be careful. Don't do this, don't do that, don't eat this… Let's face it, that's when it starts. They tell you don't do this, don't eat whatever, you know that's when it's starting, right? That's four years, John, and then when he had the second one, after that you start counting, you know? You say, okay, we're on the clock now. But what I'm sayin' is four years, figure it's four years and I'm standin' over his grave the day we buried him and I'm goin', "That's too fast." You know what I'm sayin'?

JOHN: Hey, you go seventy, seventy-odd years, I'll bet you're layin' in the bed at the end goin', "That's too fast."

BILLY: You better believe it.

JOHN: I mean your father, God bless him, he was what… sixty-five?

BILLY: Not quite.

JOHN: Still, that's not too bad.

BILLY: I'd like more.

JOHN: Hey, you and me both, brother, but I'm sayin', sixty-five, that's not too bad. I mean, hell, look at this kid. This is a sin, you know what I'm sayin'? A sin. If I'd known it was gonna be that fast, I would've come around more. Make the time. I didn't know.

BILLY: Hey, if you didn't have the time, you didn't have the time. What're you gonna do?

JOHN: I know, hey. Hey, you still seein' that girl? What's her name? With the big goo-goo eyes?

BILLY: Stel?

JOHN: Yeah, right. Stella.

BILLY: See? You'd come around, you'd know.

JOHN: It's off?

BILLY: Ah, it's friendly, but it's off. She come by, you know. I mean here. She come by last night.

JOHN: No kiddin'.

BILLY: Well, she liked the old lady. That was nice of her.

JOHN: That was.

BILLY: I mean, she didn't really know the kid. He was sick practically the whole time I knew her. It's not like she saw him much, but she always liked the old lady.

JOHN: Everybody likes the old lady. She's a peach. Sorry about Stel.

BILLY: Ah, it wasn't in the cards. What're you gonna do? It's friendly, so...

JOHN: That was nice she came.

BILLY: Yeah. You really thought she had goo-goo eyes?

JOHN: Well, you know, they were big, that's all. I'm not saying that's bad. I'm just saying they were huge.

BILLY: Huge.

JOHN: She was a cute kid, Billy. She just had big eyes. Kind of "starey."

BILLY: What's that mean? "Starey?"

JOHN: You know. She had these big, starey eyes. *John demonstrates.*

BILLY: So?

JOHN: So nothin'. I'm just sayin'. What're you gettin' all in an uproar for. You're not even seein' her anymore. *A beat.* Man, I didn't think there'd be this many people here. Well, his mother, a lot of people like his mother. Hell, they love her. She ought to run for governor.

BILLY: He had friends.

JOHN: Oh, hey, I know. I'm just sayin' it looks like a lot of people who know his mother are here.

BILLY, *pointedly:* He was a good kid, John.

JOHN: I know. What, your underwear too tight? I'm not sayin' anything.

John fumbles another cigarette out, thinks the better of it and puts it away.

BILLY: I'm glad you came. I know his mother was happy you came.

JOHN: Anybody else from the old crowd come? I saw Caruso headin' out when I was comin' in. Anybody else from the block?

BILLY: Crazy Albie. Big Fred came by. He had to work but he slipped over on his break. That was nice of him.

JOHN: Yeah, that was.

BILLY: I guess not so many, not from the corner. A few. Maybe the others'll come by tonight. You came, though.

JOHN: What, you didn't think I was gonna come?

BILLY: I just know you been busy.

JOHN: Like you wouldn't believe. Don't get me started. Hey, you think Bennie Blue's gonna come?

BILLY: Who?

JOHN: Bennie Blue. You think he's gonna come?

BILLY: Bennie Blue?

JOHN: Yeah, Bennie Blue. You don't remember Bennie Blue? Had one brown eye, one blue eye, was on "To Tell the Truth"?

BILLY: You mean BEN Blue.

JOHN: Ben Blue?

BILLY: Ben Blue. Had one brown eye, one blue eye, was on "To Tell the Truth."

JOHN: BENNIE Blue.

BILLY: BEN Blue.

JOHN: BEN Blue? Who the hell called him BEN Blue?

BILLY: I did. I thought he was dead.

JOHN: Bennie Blue?

BILLY: Ben Blue. Yeah, I heard he was dead.

JOHN: Dead?

BILLY: What, you got a hearin' problem? That's what I'm sayin'. I heard he was dead. Somebody I know – You know Little Sal? Big Sal's boy?

JOHN: Kid with the uh… *John makes a motion indicating something on his face.*

BILLY: Yeah, right, so he's helping on a wiring job on the new wing down at St. Mike's. He told me.

JOHN: You're kiddin'!

BILLY: That's what I heard.

JOHN: Jesus Christ, Bennie Blue?

BILLY: Ben Blue.

JOHN: Jesus. That another funeral I got to go to now?

BILLY: No, no. This is a while ago I heard this.

JOHN: Jesus. It's like you can't turn around. What was it? He had a heart thing, didn't he? Something with his heart?

BILLY: I don't know. I just heard he was dead.

JOHN: Jesus. Hey, there's Francis. He'll know. Hey, Francis!

Enter FRANCIS dressed in a nice, dark suit.

FRANCIS: How're you boys? John, nice to see you. *Handshake.*

JOHN: Hey, Francis. You look good.

BILLY: Hey, Francis, you did a good job, you and your people. I know his mother appreciates it.

FRANCIS: Hey, it's a closed box. We didn't do anything.

BILLY: I mean like handling the flowers and the cars and all that. I know she appreciates it. It's a nice box, too.

FRANCIS: She's a nice lady. We didn't do much but, you know, you do what you can do, right?

JOHN: Hey, Francis, remember Bennie Blue?

BILLY: BEN Blue.

FRANCIS: The guy with the eye thing?

JOHN: Was on "To Tell the Truth"?

FRANCIS: Because of his eyes?

JOHN: Billy heard he was dead.

FRANCIS: Dead?

JOHN: Yeah, this guy – Tell him, Billy. This guy –

BILLY: You know Little Sal?

FRANCIS, *indicating something on his face:* Big Sal's kid?

BILLY: He's down at St. Mike's –

FRANCIS: What's he doing down there? He okay?

JOHN: Would you shuddup and listen, Francis.

BILLY: He was doin' this wiring thing.

JOHN: He says Bennie Blue –

FRANCIS: He's not in the old man's store? I thought he was in the store.

BILLY: This is on the side. He does this on the side.

JOHN: Do you guys mind? This guy says Bennie Blue –

FRANCIS: No, no, no, he's not dead. Ben works at St. Michael's. He's not dead, though. You know who's dead? It's his BROTHER, Leo.

JOHN: Leo? Who the hell's Leo?

FRANCIS: That's the brother.

JOHN, *admonishing Billy:* The brother. *To Francis.* I didn't know Leo.

BILLY: Me neither.

JOHN: I didn't even know there was a brother.

FRANCIS: There's the two brothers. Ben's got two brothers, one older, then one older then that. Leo was the oldest. He's the one who's dead.

JOHN: You sure?

FRANCIS: I ought to be. We did Leo. Ben just works down there. Sometimes we make a run down there for a pick-up, we say hello.

JOHN: Well, next time you're down there, say hello for me.

FRANCIS: If I see him.

JOHN: Tell him John from the corner says hello.

FRANCIS: If I see him. We don't always see him. I'm not the one always making the run.

JOHN: Yeah, sure, I know. But if you see him...

FRANCIS: Yeah, sure.

JOHN: Say, "John from the corner," or he'll think it's that pinhead from the bar.

FRANCIS: If I see him, John from the corner.

BILLY: Say hello for me, too.

FRANCIS, exasperated: If I see him.

BILLY: Jeez, Francis, what're you gettin' so irritated for?

Francis answers with a glare.

FRANCIS: Hey, you guys mind if I sit?

JOHN: Sittin' down on the job, Francis?

BILLY: Might as well have a seat, Francis. They're yours. *Francis sits.*

FRANCIS: This is tough.

JOHN: Maybe you should consider another line of work.

FRANCIS: No, it's not that. THIS is tough. When you know 'em. If it's somebody I know, it's nice for them, the family, they look up and it's a friendly face going, "You need anything? You want me to send the kid out for coffee or something? You want to come lay down in the office for a bit?" I mean, you do that for everybody, but when it's somebody you know…

BILLY: Yeah.

FRANCIS: But it's tough. I don't like to do the work downstairs if it's somebody I know. I won't even go down there. But when the kid come down, well, some of them didn't want to work on him. They didn't have to do much because the box is closed, but still… well, you know…

BILLY: They get afraid.

FRANCIS: And what're you going to do? You tell them and tell them and tell them, it's okay, just be careful, but you can't make them not be afraid if they're going to be afraid. You know, they still hear stories, what can you do? Give them hell because they're afraid? So… I did the work. It's hard when it's someone you know but I felt… I don't know. I think it was good for his mother to know somebody he knew – not like I was a close friend or anything – but somebody he knew, a friend of the family… I'm glad I could tell her I wasn't too afraid to do it.

BILLY: That was nice, Francis.

FRANCIS: I hated to see him like that. You know. I knew him since he was a kid. I mean, I know the family since what?

BILLY: The year one.

FRANCIS: Yeah, the year one. I buried his grandparents. I buried his father. You know he worked for me once?

JOHN: The kid?

FRANCIS: A summer job when he was home from college. The old man was alive then, he says, "Francis, you got something, the kid can put away a few bucks for school next year?" He didn't last a day, the kid. A day. It was more like an hour. Maybe. The first body shows up and he's out of there like a shot. I mean ping! Gone! The Flash, ya know? *A beat.* Somewhere he grew up a lot. There wasn't a whole hell of a lot he was afraid of at the end. I saw him at the hospital, before they took him home. What he had to go through, the needles and all that stuff... Billy, you know.

BILLY: I know.

FRANCIS: You saw, right? This pill, that pill, this shot, that shot, three different I.V.'s... He was a good kid. I mean, I guess there was a long time he knew where it's going, right? But this last time he went into the hospital, he must've known this was the last time around, right? I was up there the day before and he could still be funny. You know, the medicine, whatever, all that stuff they were pumping into him, it made him sick. They kept a bucket there. He starts reaching for it. I grab it and hold it up for him. He smiles and he goes, "Just kidding." Just kidding, he says. He was a good kid.

BILLY: He was a good kid.

FRANCIS: You ever get up there to see him?

JOHN: I meant to.

BILLY: You know how it is.

FRANCIS: Yeah, sure. I swear, every needle they stuck in him, it was like they were taking something out instead of putting something in. When they brought him in, I see him on the table… it was like there was nothing left. You know I was the one who told her, I went to the old lady. I says, "A closed box. We can do a nice job, but it's still not going to be what it should be. He wouldn't want people to see him like that," I says. He didn't want everybody moping around –

BILLY: Like us.

FRANCIS: Yeah, exactly; like us. I says, "Look, close the box. You got pictures? Put pictures the way he was, put them up there. That's what you want people to see. I think that's what he would've wanted them to see."

BILLY: It was nice like that. You were right, Francis.

FRANCIS: I was, wasn't I? Some of the guys here were moaning but I says, "Look, it saves the old lady a few bucks – not like she cares, it's her son, right? We're out a little bit? We'll live with it." There just wasn't anything left of him. That wasn't right.

BILLY: No, the pictures were nice, doing it that way.

FRANCIS: I mean, I'm in this business a long time, guys. There's no way to make it easy. But you do what you can do.

BILLY: It was nice the way you did it.

JOHN: Hey, Francis, can I smoke up here?

FRANCIS: You have to use the room downstairs. Or you can use my office. You want to use my office? Use my office.

JOHN: I need a smoke. I'll be right back. Save my seat.

FRANCIS: If you use my office, use the Lysol when you're done. I don't want it smelling like an ashtray in there. You'll see it on the desk.

JOHN: Lysol, got it.

John and Francis stand.

FRANCIS: I should go back in, make the rounds. We'll catch up later.

Exit Francis. John hesitates then sits back down.

JOHN: I'm not gonna deodorize this guy's office. What, he thinks I'm the maid?

BILLY: What about your cigarette?

JOHN: I don't know why he's got to talk about it. Downstairs. I don't want to hear about downstairs. Do you want to hear about downstairs?

BILLY: I just think he wanted to talk.

JOHN: When I go, I want it like the Jews. They do it right. Zip, in the ground that day. Done is done.

BILLY: Yeah, but then they sit around for a week moaning about it.

JOHN: Really? A week?

BILLY: You ever hear of sitting shiva?

JOHN: Forget that, then. A week? Oof. I go, just get me in the ground, the end. Done is done.

BILLY: Well, some people –

Francis enters with DANIEL in tow.

FRANCIS: Hey, Billy. I think you know this guy. From the hospital?

Billy stands and shakes hands with Daniel.

BILLY: Yeah, yeah. Uh… *Fumbles for name.* I'm sorry…

DANIEL: Daniel.

BILLY: Yeah, that's right, Daniel. Good to see you. Dan? Danny?

DANIEL: Anything's fine.

FRANCIS: John there, he was another one of the guys from way back when. Knows the family, knew the kid all the way back.

DANIEL: Nice to meet you.

Daniel holds out his hand. John stays seated and nods a hello.

FRANCIS: Look, I have to go back in. *To Billy.* I saw him come in. I figured you'd want to say hello.

BILLY: Yeah, sure.

FRANCIS: Later, guys.

Exit Francis.

BILLY: So, Daniel, you been inside yet?

DANIEL: Yeah. His mother's a very nice lady.

BILLY: She's something. A peach, right, John?

John shrugs.

DANIEL: Somebody told me something about a box…

BILLY: Oh, yeah, well, if you got something. It's what we do, you know? Help the family.

DANIEL: Oh, I see. *Taking a few bills out of his wallet.* I didn't know. I didn't bring –

BILLY: Hey, you do what you can do. Don't worry about it, it's all right, it's fine. *Billy takes the money and puts it in the strong box. He turns the ledger to Daniel.* You sign the book. So she knows who to thank.

DANIEL: That's not necessary.

BILLY: You might as well. The old lady's gonna ask, I'm gonna tell. It'll make her feel good. *Daniel signs the book.*

DANIEL: At the hospital, when I saw her there, his mother… I'm sure it was awkward for her. You know.

BILLY: Yeah, well, you can understand that, right?

DANIEL: Oh, sure. She seems much better about it all now.

BILLY: Hey, she's a champ. I mean, you know, it's not important now. I'm sure she's glad you came. Hey, why don't you sit down?

DANIEL: Thanks.

JOHN, *standing, brusquely:* I gotta stretch my legs. I'm gonna go see who else is here. Catch you later.

Exit John. Daniel turns to Billy.

DANIEL: You sure you don't mind?

BILLY: Hey, have a seat.

They sit.

DANIEL: There was a time I used to worry about it. Should I go, should I not go. At a time like this, do you want to make people uncomfortable? They're entitled to do this the way they want. But then you're also saying to yourself, "He meant something to me, too. I want to say goodbye."

BILLY: Of course, sure. You, uh… You been to a couple of these, huh?

DANIEL: A couple.

BILLY: Sorry. That's gotta be tough. You know him a long time?

DANIEL: Not long after he finished school.

BILLY: Hey, are you the guy…

DANIEL: We had a place together.

BILLY: His mother was saying. I didn't know that was you.

DANIEL: That's me.

BILLY: No kidding.

DANIEL: Funny thing; I was trying NOT to get to know him. He was already sick when I met him, you know. But… I'm sorry, does it bother you… my talking about this?

BILLY: Hey, you want to talk, talk.

DANIEL: I didn't want to get involved with him.

BILLY: I, uh, I thought it was okay, you know, if you're careful and, uh...

DANIEL: It wasn't that. I knew what him being sick would mean... I'd been through it before.

BILLY: But you didn't stay away.

DANIEL: You knew him better than me. How could I stay away?

BILLY: Well, yeah, I guess. *Enter John, standing off, listening. Billy and Daniel don't see him.* Hey, um, his mother's having people over after. There's going to be food.

DANIEL: I know. She already invited me. I have to get back across the river before the last bus.

BILLY: Oh. Uh, you goin' to the cemetery tomorrow?

JOHN, *stepping forward:* It's usually just the family.

DANIEL: I know.

BILLY: Well, look, they're leaving from here at eleven tomorrow. If you're here, you can ride out with me. I'll get you back.

DANIEL: Thanks.

BILLY: What about you, John?

JOHN: I figure it's for the family. I'm goin' for a smoke.

Exit John. BLACKOUT. END OF SCENE 1

SCENE 2

Outside the funeral home. At rise, John paces with his cigarette. Enter Billy.

BILLY: I thought maybe you got lost.

JOHN: Nope. I'm right here.

BILLY: I thought, how long does it take for a smoke?

JOHN: Three smokes.

BILLY: I asked inside, I was lookin' for you.

JOHN: Here I am. It was like bein' inside a chimney in there, all those fat little ladies gabbin' away and puffin' like trains.

BILLY: It's cold out here. You comin' back in?

JOHN: Your little friend gone?

BILLY: He's not my "little friend," John.

JOHN: I mean, hey, was that rude or what?

BILLY: What rude?

JOHN: Why's he want to go talkin' about that stuff for? Nobody wants to hear that stuff, not here. He shouldn't be talkin' about that stuff here.

BILLY: He wanted to talk.

JOHN: You think anybody wants to hear about that here? Have a little respect, you know? Now he wants to go to the cemetery? That's for the family.

BILLY: I'M goin'.

JOHN: You know what I mean.

BILLY: Not for nothin', John, but you gotta figure, to the kid, this guy woulda been family.

JOHN: He's not family to nobody here, Billy.

BILLY: I'm just sayin', to the kid –

JOHN: He's nobody's family. I mean, Jesus, Billy, the old lady's gonna be standin' right there lookin' at this guy –

BILLY: The old lady's okay with it. She's the one who –

JOHN: The old lady's a saint, okay? What do you want from me? C'mon, Billy, it doesn't bother you? Don't tell me it doesn't bother you.

BILLY: He was what he was. What're you gonna do?

JOHN: But it bothers you, right?

BILLY: He was a good kid, John. Nothin' changes that.

JOHN: Except one thing.

BILLY: He was a good kid.

JOHN: That's what killed him, Billy.

BILLY: Hey, John, it could've been anything. He could've smoked and got cancer. He steps off a curb and gets whacked by the 29 bus. He, he –

JOHN: Not the same thing, Billy.

BILLY: Dead is dead, John.

JOHN: Not the same thing.

BILLY: He's gone. That's the thing. How come you didn't come up to the hospital?

JOHN: I told you why.

BILLY: Yeah, busy man. C'mon, you didn't want to see his friends. That it? Like this guy, Daniel –

JOHN: I told you why.

BILLY: Just so you know, John; they came. A lotta people he knew from the old days, they didn't come.

JOHN: Like me.

BILLY: I'm just sayin'. They didn't come. But this guy, Daniel, was there, and some I guess was their friends –

JOHN: All right. You want me to give 'em a medal? I shoulda come, alright? It's too late for me to say I'm sorry. It's not like he's gonna sit up and say, "Hey, John, no sweat, it's all right."

BILLY: I just wanna know was that it? Or was it him? You turned your back on him?

JOHN: I'm here, right? *A beat.* I used to say, okay, I'm a modern guy or whatever, people wanna do what they wanna do, fine, long as they don't hurt nobody and I don't have to see it. But it's not like that. You gotta deal with it and I'm tired of having to deal with it. I'm seein' the kid there, one of these guys with him… This, that, I'm tired of dealin' with it. I see him dyin' there and I see me lookin' down sayin', "Kid, you didn't have to be here."

BILLY: Half the funerals I go to I'm sayin' that. I was sayin' it when we buried my father. What happens happens. What're you gonna do? You know me. I say to myself, okay, to each his own. Whatever. But I'm like you. I get a headache just tryin' to get through the day sometimes. If it was up to me, everybody'd be straight and healthy and one color. Everybody'd live to be a hundred and they'd all get along. And if they couldn't, they wouldn't ask for alimony. But it's not up to me. Somebody wants to change the world and all that, let 'em go save the whales or somethin' over there. Tonight, for me, it's he was a good kid and he was a friend of mine. End of story. His friends come, I'll be nice to 'em because they were the kid's friends. That's all. When this is over, they go their way, I go mine. Fix the world another day. He was a good kid, John, and I want to be there to say goodbye, and if somebody else wants to say goodbye… Well, that's fine with me.

JOHN: He was a friend of mine, too, Billy.

BILLY: I know. *A beat.* Hey, look, I'm freezin' my nips off out here, I'm goin' inside. I told Francis I'd help close up.

JOHN: You leavin' from here tomorrow?

BILLY: You comin' or what?

JOHN: What time?

BILLY: We're supposed to head out around eleven.

JOHN: I ride with you?

BILLY: I'm gonna have that Daniel guy with me.

JOHN: You're such buddies, he can sit up front with you.

BILLY: See you at eleven. *Billy starts to leave, but stops.* Come on over to the old lady's house. They're havin' food. She wants you there, John. You can ride over with me.

JOHN: What the hell. It's cold out here. *They start to exit together.* He was a good kid, wasn't he, Billy?

BILLY: Best there ever was.

FADE TO BLACK

CURTAIN

END OF PLAY

LAST DANCE

Carol Schlanger

LAST DANCE was first produced by the Haven Artistic Collective in New York City, under the banner of "The Mercy Plays" (2006). The show was directed by April Nickell and featured John Harrison and Lindsey Gee.

CAST OF CHARACTERS

MARLENE: *Female, 40's -50's*
JUMP: *Male, Late 20's - early 30's*
SUE LEE: *Female, Late 20's - early30's*

SETTING:

A Dance Class

THE TIME:

Late Afternoon. The Present.

NOTES for *Last Dance*

Zydeco dance steps are easily discovered on the net and exact replication is not necessary. The music need not be by Noony and the Floaters, but should be very peppy with a New Orleans Zydeco flavor.

Peppy ZYDECO music: It's "Noony and the Floaters." A young couple dances across the stage to the music. They are terrific. They dance off. Down music.

At rise, a bare stage. MARLENE, a sad-eyed woman in her early-fifties stands opposite a semi-circle of about ten, cardboard cutout MEN (also can be projected on video screen). The men are of varying age, size, and ethnicity and can be presented in detail or as blank shapes. In the center of the semi-circle stands JUMP, a bright-eyed cowboy in his early-thirties. The map of Ireland is clearly etched on Jump's smiling face. The ZYDECO music is turned up a notch. Jump instructs the group, but the audience and Marlene understand that he's speaking directly to her.

JUMP, *demonstrating:* And step, hold, brush, slide. And step, hold, brush, slide.

MARLENE, *as she copies his steps, she talks to AUDIENCE and to herself:* This is fun… maybe.

JUMP: You got it! Step, hold, brush, slide. That's it. That's it!

MARLENE: I got it.

JUMP: Together now, with the basic! *Demonstrating.* Quick, quick, slow. Quick, quick, slow.

MARLENE, *following his new move:* I have a dishwasher, but I don't use it. I just let the dishes pile up in the sink and then wash them by hand.

JUMP: Okay now, let's give it a whirl. *He whirls.* And put a little spit and shine on!

MARLENE: The warm water feels so good on my hands. *She tries to whirl, but doesn't cut it.* What if I had to flee America with no time to take anything and go to a country where I couldn't speak the language?

JUMP: There you go! And quick-quick-slow, quick-quick-slow, step-hold-brush-slide. Good! Again!

MARLENE: I'd have to labor like an immigrant. Clean rich people's houses. People who have money have houses that have no smell, did you ever notice that?

JUMP: Together now with the spin out! On the "One" foot…

MARLENE: And when the rich people came home, they'd track dirt on my clean floors, emit bad odors in the bathroom, and then I'd have to start all over. Otherwise things could get rank and they'd realize that they were stinky like the rest of us.

JUMP: And step, hold, brush… slide and spin! *Marlene spins. She's more adept this time.* Great! Ladies, if you don't have a partner raise your hand! *Marlene raises her hand.* Well, go git one!

The Zydeco music comes up. Marlene takes the hand of the first cardboard man and accidentally steps on his foot.

MARLENE: I'm SO sorry. I'm new at this. Spaghetti arms? Oh, noodley. Soft, like a wet noodle. *She tightens her arms.* Marlene…

JUMP: Everybody hooked up? Don't be shy!

MARLENE: Sorry. My arm goes over your neck. This is my very first time… Chuck. *To Us.* My hand is shaking. I hope Chuck doesn't notice. *To CHUCK.* From Valencia? I never met anyone from Valencia before. Great orange country, right? I love fresh orange juice, the kind with the bits still in. Not reconstituted. *To Us.* I never shook before. Not before the terrible, worst thing that ever happened, happened. *She twirls as she speaks to Chuck.* Yes, I am married but my husband didn't come. He doesn't enjoy dancing. If I had one word of advice to give a younger woman, I'd say, don't marry a man who won't dance.

JUMP: You all are turnin' into real swamp stompers!

MARLENE: I'm from Michigan, originally. Dearborn. Home of the double pronged forklift. The air in Dearborn is metallic, it smells like aluminum foil.

JUMP: And change partners!

MARLENE: Bye now, Chuck. No. I'm not a friend of Bill W. Who's he? *Marlene moves on to another cardboard man, BYRON. He's shorter than she is.* Marlene. Nice to meet you too, Byron. I like your tie. I can almost smell those red roses. Oh. Brut... I had a friend in college who wore...

JUMP: And now the lovely Sue Lee Whippet will join me in demonstrating the thigh thrust lean in. Sue EEEEE!!!

SUE LEE enters and runs Center Stage. Her thighs are strong enough to clamp down on any bull, real or mechanical. Jump grabs her, spins her around, and dips her into a backbend. Sue Lee loves it. Marlene claps but without enthusiasm.

SUE LEE: I'd bend over fer you anytime, Jump.

JUMP: Lord love you, Sue Lee! *Sue Lee and Jump demonstrate.* Now on my "One" foot, I slide back and Sue Lee steps forward on her "Two" foot. Everybody remember which is their "One" and which is their " Two." If ya do, let's hear it!

MARLENE: Yes, Jump. I do.

SUE LEE: Louder, don't hear ya!

MARLENE: I remember!

JUMP: Good! *Demonstrating.* My hand goes right up against the small of Sue Lee's back. Tight and strong.

It is obvious that Jump and Sue Lee have the following banter down pat.

SUE LEE: I hope nobody takes this next thing we're about to tell ya as anti-feminism or anything.

JUMP: Cause Zydeco's number one rule is as old as Adam and Eve, and we all know that Adam came first and then Eve jes popped out his side, kinda like an afterthought.

SUE LEE: What'd I just say, Jump?

JUMP: Shoot. You don't give an inch, do you Sue Lee?

SUE LEE: Nope. But I do hope you do, Jump. Maybe even three or four.

JUMP: You're just asking for it. Ain't ya, honey?

SUE LEE: Better n' beggin'.

JUMP: Zydeco's number one rule is... everybody listening?

MARLENE: I'm all ears, Jump.

JUMP: Zydeco's number one rule is: "The Man Always Leads." Okay fellas, you got that?

SUE LEE: Now as Jump's foot comes forward, mine goes back.

Jump pushes his leg between Sue Lee's thighs.

JUMP: Then we snake on down.

Sue Lee and Jump snake to the floor, each topping the other in their strong sexual moves.

SUE LEE: Okay, now everybody. Your turn...

Marlene tries to snake: It's a disaster, she kicks Byron.

MARLENE: I'm so sorry, Chuck. Oh. Byron. I mean Byron. I hope I didn't hurt you. I get clumsy sometimes. You're a doctor. Really? From Tacoma? Okay, I'll try it. I'll try Byron but I don't think my knee will reach that high because I can't get down very low. *She bends down on one leg and lifts her knee which touches Byron's crotch.* Hey, don't thank me. Stop rubbing against my knee like that. Stop it, Byron! Get away from there! Of all the nerve!!

She backs away, still trying to keep the beat.

JUMP: You're all getting' hotter n' fresh tar.

MARLENE, *to Byron:* Wrong! I didn't like it, Byron. Not one bit. I hated it and I don't think you care about learning to dance at all! What you did was like our old horny dog before he was spayed. You did too! No, I don't want to sit at your table at dinner, my son is dead.

SUE LEE: Everybody switch! Change yer partner.

MARLENE: Byron. Bye. And you just watch yourself.

Marlene moves to the next man.

SUE LEE: Let's go, everybody! Move on down the line.

JUMP: Life's like that.

SUE LEE: You tell 'em, Jump. Now everybody, don't forget yer basics. Step, hold, brush, and slide. Step, hold, brush, and slide.

MARLENE: Hi, Mike. I'm Marlene. Nice to meet you, too. My son is dead, he caught some shrapnel in his head. No, it's not Country Western song. Hank Williams did? Really? I never heard of it.

JUMP: And turn. Everybody, turn. Don't forget those arms. Keep em' hard.

Marlene turns and then comes back to Mike.

SUE LEE: Practice what you preach now, Jump.

MARLENE: Mike, we're getting it! In a Humvee. He had no protection on his side and it came through the window. Just like that. Metal exploding his skull. It cracked it right in half. They had no right to send him out that way. The army…

JUMP, *to Sue Lee:* Girl, when's the last time someone whooped your bottom?

MARLENE, *to Mike:* His very best friend was driving. He called to tell us that my son tried to speak, to say something, but my son couldn't; not one word. His brain was splattered all over the seat, like scrambled eggs. All moist and convoluted with little bumps and fissures, stinking like the devil's own rotten sulfur. *She twirls.* And just those wondrous dark brown eyes looking up, with lashes so long; he was born with long, thick lashes. So big and strong and handsome, so twenty-two fresh like new alfalfa grass. Every time I looked at him I thought I was a miracle maker.

JUMP: Okay, now we're gonna up the pace a little, just double up. *Jump and Sue Lee clap to a faster beat.* One, two, three, four, slide, hold, brush, slide and one, two, three, four.

SUE LEE: Get down, y'all! Get down!

Jump and Sue Lee really start to move. Marlene quickens her pace.

MARLENE, *to Mike:* My boy… Young men are so beautiful. Like brilliant colored birds. *She does a double twirl.* We are getting pretty good!

JUMP: Okay now, one of you lucky ladies are gonna get a chance with the master, yours truly. Any volunteers?

SUE LEE: Come on girls, don't be shy. Once you try him, I promise you, you'll like it.

A long beat.

JUMP: Sue Lee, looks like I'm jes gonna have to pick! *He grabs Marlene, as Sue Lee moves towards a cut-out man.* Come on down!

MARLENE: No… really, Jump.

JUMP: You can do it, darlin'. Jes put your self in the hands of the ole Jumpster. What's yer name again?

MARLENE: Marlene.

JUMP: We got a Marlene in the house! Marlene, you're in for one smooth ride. *Jump and Marlene dance. She's really catching on. Her face lights up.* Now, I'm gonna do the "Throw-out." Everybody watching? Ready, Marlene?

MARLENE: I guess.

Jump throws Marlene away from him, brings her back and twirls her.

MARLENE, *girlishly:* Steve, you're right. This is really so much fun!

Jump repeats the "Throw-Out" with Marlene. They dance smoothly. For a brief moment, Marlene is transformed. Her movements become graceful and joyous.

MARLENE: The hairs are just standing up on my neck, I'm so excited. When you first asked me out, I thought, "Nooo, he's not my type." But look at us now!

JUMP: Now darlin'. . .

MARLENE: Honestly, Steve, this is the best first date I've ever been on. I'm very cautious, you know, most college guys that ask me out are so childish, especially the ones in your frat, Zeta Beta whatever. Somebody ought to tell them they wear too much Canoe cologne... but not you. I'm so glad. I knew there was something about you...

JUMP: Darlin', I'm not Steve.

MARLENE: I can do this again next weekend, Steve. That is, if you like. I'm free n'all.

JUMP: Honey pie, I'm Jump.

MARLENE: Who?

JUMP: Jump. Your Zydeco teacher.

MARLENE, *deflated:* Oh. He's my husband. Steve. Twenty-three years.

JUMP, *back on automatic:* Youbetcha! One more time, the "Throw-Out" everybody. Trick is to keep those arms stiff. And guys, you lead with yer "One" leg. Here we go!

He throws Marlene again, but this time, she stumbles to the floor. Sue Lee and Jump help her to her feet.

SUE LEE: You all right, sweetheart?

MARLENE: My son's dead.

SUE LEE: Sorry to hear that.

MARLENE: In Iraq. He was about your age, Jump. My sweet, sweet boy.

SUE LEE: Maybe you jes better take a little break, hon.

MARLENE: Every morning, just after I wake up, I forget, but then I remember. The days go and come. I see people and hear things, but they aren't really there. They're ghosts. Ghost people eating ghost dinner rolls before the waiter with the fish mouth tells them that the osso bucco is excellent...

JUMP: Okay, everybody! You gotta fall down if you want to git up, right Marlene?

MARLENE: Yes. I know that, but not...

JUMP: Cause we're all here at Zydeco Dance Camp to let loose and try something brand spankin' new. If our feet keep movin', the rest of us ain't far behind. You go on back now, Marlene. Everybody, let's give the little lady a big, big Zydeco hand. *Jump leads Marlene back to the circle with a flourish. Sue Lee claps wildly.* Ready to show em' the "Drop-Sit," Sue Lee?

SUE LEE: Ready as I'll ever be, Jump.

JUMP: Okay. You guys are lookin' good... real good. So here's the "Drop-Sit." On the "One" foot, the ladies spin out. The gentlemen bend their "Two" foot and pull yer girl back onto yer knee.

He demonstrates with Sue Lee. Marlene tries the step with her next cut-out partner.

MARLENE: Orin from Miami? I'm Marlene. I hope I'm not too heavy for you, Orin. My son, my Gary… my Gary, he trained in Florida… Pensacola. The heat didn't get to him cause he was so very dark. Over there, in Fallujah, they thought he was Greek or Turkish or something. That's how he was born, dark and smooth, like an olive.

The music rises, drowning out everything as Jump, Sue Lee, and Marlene keep on dancing.

BLACKOUT

END OF PLAY

THE SELLING OF THE SOUL

Walter Dalton

It's 2009. We are in a conference room of Rogers, Unger & Finkle-stein, a large Madison Ave. Advertising Agency. In the ad business, they're known as RUF. A large conference table sits in the middle of the stage. A large presentation stand with blank, butcher paper faces the table. TYLER MORRIS, a young Creative-Director whiz stands in front of the presentation stand holding a big, black marking pen. Around the table sit two eager writer/art director teams with pads and pens. Tyler, the latest young, Industry hotshot is wearing his hair in an Afro.

TYLER: As I'm sure you all know by now, Rogers, Unger and Finklestein Or-

Extending his arm for a response.

ALL: Ruff... Ruff... Ruff...

TYLER: That's right. Ruff has acquired the Positive Plus account. Hey, J.Walter Thomson... BITE ME... Okay? *Everyone screams their approval.* We are gonna kick some serious ass here for Positive Plus... or as I call the... Double P. *The two teams begin chanting cheer-leading style.* DOUBLE P RUFF RUFF... DOUBLE P RUFF RUFF... WHO'S RUFF? WE'RE RUFF, DOUBLE P RUFF RUFF!

TYLER: They're number four, but folks we're gonna make them number one! *Enthusiastic reaction.* Sorry Right Guard, Ban, and Secret. Your ship has sailed! Now, I want everyone to start thinking deodorant. That's right. We are in the pit-paste bidness!

DOCHERTY: Let's create a new neurosis for the sheep.

TYLER: Good one, Doc. What fear did for tire sales, insecurity can do for Deodorant. *Turning towards the stand and writing... Neurosis.* Question? Who's our target? Or should I say... Tar... Zay. Talk to me, Jen-hen.

JENNIFER BROWN, *reading from her stat sheet:* Marketing analysis research says P.P.'s selling appeal is to women between the ages of 24 and 31 and three quarters. General income bracket. High... skewers towards WASP... light on low minority. Daytime exposure. Perfect soap opera and reality-based prime-time.

TYLER, *writing furiously:* Wasp... low min... heavy soap... soft real... Pri-Tie. Good one, Brownie.

MORGAN: And Dude, people in that income bracket tend to buy more nylon-based material as opposed to cotton and that can only lead you to... *Singing...* sweat street.

TYLER: Kick ass and take names, Morgan!

DOCHERTY: Now stop me if you heard this, but aren't these chicks buying P.P. for the whole family? Right? In other words, it might be a big mistake to make a female approach only. Let's get them embar-rassed about not only their perspiration, but lard ass over there with the remote and the zombie kids playing Grand Theft Auto. Am I right, folks?

TYLER, *writing feverishly:* On target, Doc man. Great... keep it coming... Hubby... kids... I love it! We're cookin', kids... target in sight. Now. Execution...

JENNIFER: What about a talking armpit?

TYLER: Not bad. Not bad. *He writes out "talking armpit."* What would it say?

DOCHERTY, *dramatically:* "Stop me, please someone stop me before I stink more."

MORGAN, *correcting her:* Smell more.

DOCHERTY, *raising his voice:* Stink more!

TYLER, *to Jennifer:* Stat!

JENNIFER, *quickly going thru her research till she strikes gold:* "Stink more" is 47 % more effective than "smell more" if the demographic is forty-plus white male... middle range income. "Smell more plays better to mid-range white women... minorities are a push."

TYLER, *writing stink... smell:* Use 'em both...more ideas.

JENNIFER: How 'bout the talking "arm-pitt" and Brad Pitt?

TYLER, *writing:* Brad Pitt...more...

MORGAN: Bret Favre... use that whole Green Bay Affair... *In a Southen drawl.* They don't want me in Green Bay? That makes me sweat. But with Positive Plus, I'm dry and I know I'll play somewhere...

TYLER, *writing:* Sports Star... nice direction. *Stops writing.* Keep the train on the track, folks.

DOCHERTY: Hollywood, get Clooney and Damon to rip off an old Hope and Crosby road movie. *Beat.* On the road to Sweatsville...

MORGAN, *with venom:* Or maybe something in this fuckin' century...

TYLER: I'm listening.

MORGAN: We can rip off Newman and Hanks.

TYLER: *Nice vein, to Jennifer*: Numbers?

JENNIFER: Clooney will only do Japanese with a five mil guarantee and Damon will jump aboard if we get George.

TYLER: Have legal call ICM and see if Clooney will dance if we give him stock and a small ownership. And at the same time check Brad Pitt's availability.

JENNIFER: Done.

TYLER: Slogans?

MORGAN: Positive Plus stops perspiration fuss…

TYLER, *writing:* Good.

DOCHERTY: "No sweat, man."

JENNIFER: We hire a midget family… documentary style. Don't sweat the small stuff???

TYLER: Any midget stars?

MORGAN: Verne Troyer.

TYLER: Who?

MORGAN: He played Mini-Me in the Austin Powers Franchise.

TYLER: Not big enough. Pardon the pun! *Writing out Mini-Me.* That's a tough sell…

MORGAN: We get a Sir Edmund Hillary look-a-like to scale Mt. Everest… on top, he looks to camera and says… "Positive Plus… because it's there."

TYLER, *writing:* Screw Mt… Everest… we shoot it in Canada…

Lights Fade & music does a flash back musical interlude. Lights Come Up… Same conference room NINE YEARS EARLIER. The presentation board is clean and the same creative staff await the entrance of the then young whiz kid creative director, Docherty. The actor who plays Tyler has lost the Afro and is now playing J.D. THOMAS, a talented but worn-out, older, cynical alcoholic. On lights up, Docherty makes his appearance and heads straight towards the presentation board. The other staff are anxious and nervous.

DOCHERTY: Well, I just got off the phone with Dick Cheney... *A dramatic beat.* And we WON! RUF is the agency that is going to make George Bush the next President of these here United States of America. *A loud CHEER goes up... The group break into the CHEER we heard earlier, all except J.D. Thomas, who sits perfectly still.*

DOCHERTY/JENNIFER/MORGAN: GEORGIE BUSH... RUF RUF... GEORGIE BUSH... RUF RUF... WHO'S RUF... WE'RE RUF... GEORGIE BUSH... RUF RUF.

Doc holds up his hands, silencing the group.

DOCHERTY: Now then...

J.D. THOMAS: Big fuckin' deal...

DOCHERTY: Mr. Thomas, are you going to be able to work on this account?

J.D. THOMAS: Son, I've got three ex-wives and a bar bill bigger than some Third world countries... *A beat.* Just tell me what you want me to do, but don't expect any rah-rah bullshit.

DOCHERTY: Deal. Talk to me, people.

JENNIFER: What's our direction? Is he really a conservative?

DOCHERTY: Cheney says he's anything you want him to be. *In a Cheney voice.* "Just get the sombitch elected."

J.D. THOMAS, *with venom:* He's as dumb as a bag of hammers.

DOCHERTY: Cheney says he doesn't read...

J.D. THOMAS: Or write.

DOCHERTY: Moving ahead. He's got a terrific memory for names, but he's nervous in front of a camera.

MORGAN: Is he the best horse they got?

DOCHERTY: Karl Rove told me just make him look good. Babies, baseball, and apple pie... he'll do the rest.

JENNIFER: Compassionate Conservatism... a little religion, a lot of right wing.

DOCHERTY, *writing it down:* Good. Good.

J.D. THOMAS: How bout... "The guy who's fucked up every job he's ever had?"

DOCHERTY: Stay positive.

J.D. THOMAS: All right. I'm positive he's fucked up every job he's ever had.

MORGAN: "Real Plans for Real People."

DOCHERTY: Good. Maybe show him on his ranch baling hay, working with the animals... Heartland hero... I like it.

J.D. THOMAS: Hero? What the fuck's he ever done?

DOCHERTY: Governor of Texas.

J.D. THOMAS: Paid and bought for by Daddy Bush. Or maybe highlight his cheerleading experiences or daddy buying him part ownership in the Texas Rangers, where he lost them a whole bunch of… money. Or maybe the fact that he put more prisoners to death than any other state in the nation.

Just then a Rod Serling look-a-like walks to center stage, lights up a cigarette, and addresses the audience. A spotlight hits Rod while the others continue their brainstorming in mime and in shadows.

ROD: Witness if you will... Advertising Executives. Glib, quasi-hip, high-energy, word/visual freaks who think of themselves as important elements in the day-to-day business of what America does best... selling! Crap! Fancy a brain-dead President? Or perhaps the new gas-guzzling SUV rolling off the line at General Motors? Or maybe you'd like to clog your arteries with that tasty treat from KFC which combines gravy, cheese, and greasy fried chicken. If it's crap... we can sell it... because you will buy it! *A beat.* I'm Rod Serling of "The Twilight Zone." I'm not dead. Worse, I'm in reruns. We're on the Turner Network every Friday at midnight. And for 78.85 you can buy the whole first season. And…if you call in now, you'll get a free t-shirt. *Rod holds up a t-shirt that says "I GOT STONED IN THE TWILIGHT ZONE."* And be sure to book your reservation on The Twilight Zone... Cruise to Craziness. I'll be there selling t-shirts and Rod Serling ties and even autographed cigarettes. *He takes a big inhale.* Remember kids… it's cool to smoke. *He exits.* This is a great fuckin' gig!

CURTAIN

JETTISON

Brendan Andolsek Bradley

JETTISON, by Brendan Andolsek Bradley; Commissioned in March of 2007 by the Impetuous Theater Group and Joe Cecala for the SWIM SHORTS 3 Festival. Directed by Brian P. Leahy; Vessel custom built in Nebraska by Brendan Bradley; Technical Direction by Joseph Powell; Special thanks to Don Bradley for helping drive the boat cross country in 23 hours. Opening Night was July 18, 2007 at the rooftop swimming pool of the Midtown Manhattan Holiday Inn, 440 West 57th Street.

STARRING

GARY: STEVE T. SMITH
STEVE: BRYCE GILL
BOB: CLAYTON DEAN SMITH

The Pacific Ocean. Day. A small, life boat floats on open water occupied by three distressed men. They are unshaven, overexposed to the sun, and their clothes are ragged. STEVE, a shirtless, hunky day trader sleeps surrounded by empty beer bottles. BOB, a tired and grey middle-aged man wears a tattered Hawaiian shirt and khakis, is dozing heavily. GARY, on "lookout duty" wears a life preserver and collects crumbs from the floor of the boat into his bulky coat. He mumbles quietly to himself...

GARY: It's okay. We're okay. Just a little while longer...

STEVE, *sitting up:* Whaddya got there?

GARY: Nothing.

STEVE: Nice try, shit-dick. Is that food?

GARY: No.

STEVE: I'm sorry, Mumbles, what was that? Give it here.

GARY: Stop!

STEVE, *mocking:* Oh! Stop!

GARY: You're gonna capsize us!

STEVE: Whaddya, afraid?

GARY: I can't swim, asshole!

STEVE: "I can't swim, asshole!" Then give me whatever the fuck you're hiding.

BOB, *rising:* Steve, stop.

STEVE: Oh, c'mon!

GARY: You should be a nicer person.

STEVE, *to Bob:* We need to talk.

BOB: Steve.

STEVE: Right now!

Bob considers the request and then looks at Gary apologetically. Gary sighs and knowingly turns around in his seat so that he faces the other direction with his back to them. Bob and Steve wait for Gary to fully turn around and then huddle where they are standing, to conspire privately as if they are behind closed doors.

STEVE, *continued:* This is ridiculous. He's hiding shit. I know it. I just saw him sneaking something into his jacket.

BOB: Steve, you know there is no more food.

STEVE: 'Cause fuckwad stole it all.

BOB: No. We all shared the rations evenly, from the beginning. He couldn't possibly have anything we don't know about.

STEVE: I'm not messing around. I can smell it on him. I'm fucking hungry!

BOB: We're all hungry, Steve. None of us expected to run out of food.

STEVE: Was that really all you could manage to salvage from the "Pride of Aloha"?

BOB: Oh, no. Actually the kitchen was just littered with boxes of dry and canned goods pre-packed with itemized lists, right next to the handy GPS system and keys to the escape chopper, but my tennis arm was a little sore, so I left most of it behind to allow a fair shot to everyone else. What do you think? *Gary snickers to himself. Steve turns at the noise.*

STEVE: The fuck you laughing at?

GARY: Bob's funny when he's dehydrated.

STEVE: You better –

BOB: Gary, please buddy.

STEVE: Yeah, this is a private fucking conversation.

GARY: It's not like I can't hear you.

STEVE: Then stop listening.

GARY: Where do you want me to go?

STEVE: Are you offering?

BOB: Guys, please! Can we handle this like adults?

STEVE: Thanks, Mom.

BOB: Listen, Gary. I believe you. I know you have nothing to hide from us. But we've been out here a lot longer than any of us expected-

Bob is interrupted by the satisfying crack of a bottle top being pried open. Steve has retrieved a beer from his stash in the boat and popped off using the hull of the vessel. Bob turns and Steve offers the beer innocently. Bob returns a disapproving look and continues.

BOB: And if we're going to survive together, we have to accommodate each other's delightful quirks and needs. I think this is ridiculous too, but please... let's just indulge Steve for a moment and remove your jacket, show us there's nothing there, and then we can resume our very busy lives of baking and drifting into oblivion.

GARY: I can't.

Steve growls at Gary, violently grabbing him by his collar. Bob attempts to break it up.

STEVE: The hell you can't. Show me what you're hiding!

BOB: Steve!

GARY: NO! STOP IT! Okay! ALRIGHT! I'll do it. *Trembling, Gary carefully unfastens his life jacket and hands it to Bob. He opens his bulky coat and slowly reveals a small, white bunny. Bob and Steve stare, speechless. A long beat.*

GARY, *continued:* He's my friend.

BOB: How did you –

STEVE: Food.

BOB: Why didn't you –

STEVE: Food!

GARY: Can we keep him? *Beat. Both Steve and Bob, confused and shocked, try to gain control of themselves.*

STEVE: We need to talk.

BOB: Okay.

STEVE: Right the fuck now!

GARY: I'm not turning around.

STEVE: You fucking lied! You don't have a say in the matter!

GARY: It's my bunny!

BOB: Steve! He's right. This involves all of us. Gary, where did you get the rabbit?

GARY: When the ship was going down, I was so scared. The walls groaned as the water leaked from the ceiling. The gasping sirens echoed to evacuate "in a calm, orderly fashion." I guess the will to survive takes over, right Steve? Bob grabbed as much food as he could carry. Steve raided the bar. But me...I just panicked. As I ran for the top deck, I found this little guy. He looked so pale and fluffy frozen in the middle of the corridor.

STEVE: Yeah, like a fucking marshmallow. Let's mangia.

GARY, *ignoring Steve:* I never really thought about where he came from, but I just knew I had to save him. I scooped him into my pocket and kept running. Our first few days on the water, I just coddled him, mostly to comfort myself. But after we lost Lisa – sorry, Bob – I knew I couldn't tell anyone. He's all I have and I'm going to get him out of this.

BOB: Gary. You have a rabbit.

STEVE: A fucking rabbit.

GARY: I'm sorry.

STEVE: No, you're not. But you will be.

BOB: All this time. We're going to die out here. Do you understand that? No one is coming. We haven't eaten in six days. I didn't know my body could do that, but I doubt it can do it much longer. I'm not saying we could actually eat him, but Jesus, Gary! Look at me! Would you let Steve die? *An uncomfortable pause.* Okay, would you watch me die? Starve? Rot in the sun? All so you can save – *Beat. Bob realizes Gary might rather keep the rabbit than his shipmates.*

BOB: Oh, you didn't name him, did you?

GARY: Fluffernutter.

BOB: Well, it's not Harvey.

STEVE: Christ, I'm hungry!

BOB: Come here. *Gary shuffles a little closer and suspiciously passes the Rabbit to Bob. Bob cradles the rabbit like an infant.*

STEVE: What are you doing? Am I the only one who hasn't lost his fucking mind? Anyone heard of rabbit stew?

BOB, *to the rabbit:* Hey, buddy. Yeah, you've had quite an adventure, huh? I'll bet you're hungry, yeah. And tired. And scared.

STEVE: Haasenpfeffer? Rabbit under a glass? Anyone?

GARY: We can't kill him.

BOB: Steve, could we really kill something?

Steve's silence answers the question. We watch him battle within himself and finally give in.

STEVE: Here, let me see Roger, darling. *Bob hesitates knowingly.* C'mon. Trust me. *Bob carefully passes the rabbit into Steve's clumsy hands. Steve lifts the rabbit into the air above his head and baby talks.* Well, hey there mister. Look at you! You are kinda cute, huh? Everyone's making such a fuss over you. *Steve "flies" the bunny toward Gary menacingly. Singing...* Little Bunny Foo Foo, I just wanna see you, sizzling in a sauce pan, and melting in my mouth. *Gary desperately lurches for his rabbit. Steve teases him further by opening his mouth and inserting the bunny's head inside.*

GARY: GIVE HIM BACK!

BOB: Steve! Put him down. We haven't decided anything yet. *Steve surrenders the rabbit like a victorious older brother returning a stolen toy. He opens another beer off the side of the boat, takes a long, magnificent chug, and exhales proudly.* We need to handle this civilly. *Beat.* We should vote on it.

STEVE: Vote.

BOB: I think it's best if we handle this democratically.

STEVE: Fuck Democracy! We are in a boat in the middle of fucking nowhere. None of us have eaten for, what, a week! And Houdini here produces Rabbit Fricassee and you want to introduce the electoral fucking process!

BOB: Steve.

STEVE: No. I absolutely see your point. I mean, what would PETA say? Yeah, we should just tough it out. You know, Bob, like Lisa. She was a sport, huh?

GARY: Don't you dare bring her into this!

STEVE, *going for the kill:* Gee Bob, I wonder how keen you'd be on keeping Thumper here if you were still holding your dying wife in your fucking arms!

GARY: Stop talking!

STEVE, *barking:* MAKE ME, YOU FUCK!

Steve attacks Gary, grabbing for the rabbit. They struggle ferociously, rocking the boat. Bob attempts to separate them. Their dialogue overlaps.

STEVE: You ate all the fucking food Bob brought. I've shared my beer. IT'S YOUR TURN, MOTHER FUCKER! You have to contribute to the group. I'll kill you too if I have to, but I AM NOT GONNA FUCKING DIE! NOW GIVE ME THE FUCKING RABBIT!

GARY: Get your hands off of me! You're not taking him. LET GO! He's mine and I'm not letting anything happen to him!

BOB: STOP IT! Steve! Gary! I'VE HAD IT WITH BOTH OF YOU! This rodent's caused nothing but problems. It's not a goddamn pet or a meal – IT'S A FUCKING CURSE! *Bob pulls away from the tangle, grasping the rabbit in his arms. He is fighting for breath and at the end of his wits. Bob pulls back and hurls the rabbit with all his strength into the water. Catching his breath.* THERE! Now no one gets the rabbit!

STEVE: What the hell have you done?

GARY: No!

STEVE: That was all we had, you son of a bitch!

GARY: NO!

STEVE: That was our last fucking chance! How could you throw away our last fucking chance? *Gary throws himself clumsily into the water after the rabbit and fights awkwardly to swim, but realizes he is only sinking. Blinded by rage, Steve grabs Bob by the throat and begins choking him furiously, not noticing Gary's struggle.* You idiot! You stupid, fucking moron! I'm not gonna starve out here alone! Do you hear me? I'm gonna be the one that makes it. *Bob gives the last of his fight, but quickly suffocates and sinks into the bottom of the boat.*

Gary is barely treading water, crying out, and desperately scanning the surface.

GARY: Bob! Help! I can't! *Steve realizes what he's done and notices Gary for the first time. He panics, looking for something to throw to Gary.*

STEVE: Gary! No!

GARY: Do… do you see him?

STEVE: What? Gary, just hold on.

GARY: I'm sorry. I was supposed to save him.

Gary slips under the surface of the water and disappears for twenty seconds. When his body emerges, it is floating limp, dead. Steve surveys the two bodies and scans the entire horizon for some sign of help. He sinks to his seat in the middle of the vessel, fully taking in the sequence of events. Absent mindedly, Steve fumbles opens a beer and begins drinking. On his second sip, something catches his eye… a few feet from the boat. Steve sees the rabbit swimming back to the boat. Gently, Steve crouches at the side of the boat and lovingly scoops the shivering creature into his arms. He cradles the rabbit and scans the horizon one last time...

STEVE, *softly:* It's okay. We're okay. Just a little while longer…

THE END

4 DAYS IN BED

Jonson Kuhn
and
Ariel Marks

4 DAYS IN BED was originally produced by Kurt Lewis in June of 2008 at the Crossroads Theatre in Denver, CO. It was directed by Jonson Kuhn and featured Patrick Ryan and Ariana Griffith in the starring roles.

CHARACTERS

DENVER: *Man in his mid-twenties.*

TUCSON: *Woman in her early thirties.*

SETTING:

DENVER's bedroom.

TIME:

Present day. Denver, Colorado.

NOTES for *4 Days In Bed*

Takes place essentially over four days – Saturday to Monday Night.

SCENE 1
SATURDAY NIGHT *around 8pm*

Bedroom, night. Spotlight hits the bed and finds DENVER *and* TUCSON *in bed passionately making out while "La Vie En Rose" plays in the background. They kiss for a good while until she breaks loose.*

TUCSON: How have you been?

DENVER: Good.

TUCSON: Your hair's longer.

DENVER: Yeah.

Immediately they go back to making out as the song plays out a little longer and then dims out with the lights. End of Scene.

SCENE 2
LATER SATURDAY NIGHT

Later that night, Denver and Tucson are smoking in bed.

DENVER: I'm a stallion!

TUCSON: Hmm.

DENVER: I'm telling you, I'm in some kinda zone. It's been a while.

TUCSON: In the past year?

DENVER: Less than that.

TUCSON: How long?

DENVER: I don't know, a while.

TUCSON: A while… what? Weeks? Months?

DENVER: Months.

TUCSON: Me too. Well, a few. You know I was on that whole born-again virgin streak until after you left Tucson last summer. So you're out of practice?

DENVER: I'm in training… seasonal training. Tonight was fine, but I don't know what happens – sometimes everything works just fine…other times, not so much. For a while, I just assumed it had something to do with the smoking, but then like I went to the gas station and saw how high the price of gas was and I thought, "No, THIS is the problem." How can anybody be expected to maintain a hard-on when gas is damn near four bucks a gallon?

TUCSON: I was reading a Cosmo on the plane…

DENVER: Why?

TUCSON: I don't know. The only time I ever buy it is when I'm in the airport – you know how the airport depresses me – I needed something trashy and indulgent to read. I can see how gas prices might make it difficult for a guy to get it up, or keep it up, but Cosmo says the number one reason men have trouble performing in the bedroom is because they won't feel a connection with their partner – like their heart won't be in it. I've always thought that men could like erect themselves on command, you know, like just tune into the Victoria's Secret catalog in their heads or something.

DENVER: You sure there wasn't anything in there about gas prices?

TUCSON: I don't know. I didn't finish the whole article. By the way, I wanted to say thanks again for picking me up.

DENVER: My pleasure.

TUCSON: I liked that you came in and met me inside. Nobody ever does that.

DENVER: Exactly. That's why I did it. Every time I come back in through that airport, I see all these people standing by the fountain waiting for someone. I've always wanted someone waiting there for me.

TUCSON: I'd wait for you by the fountain.

DENVER: That's all I've ever wanted to hear. *Pause.* So… four days in the big city. You got anything in particular you wanna do – wanna see?

TUCSON: I wanna check out a meeting while I'm out here.

DENVER: Oh, yeah, the AA – I remember.

TUCSON: Did you remember to look anything up for me?

DENVER: Yyyeeesss?

TUCSON: So, no?

DENVER: I've been busy.

TUCSON: You've been unemployed.

DENVER: And that takes up a lot of time. More than you'd think. Now that I actually have a job, I've never felt so… not busy in my life.

TUCSON: I'll find one for myself, don't worry about it.

DENVER: Well, what else? You don't want to spend four days going to AA meetings, do you?

TUCSON: No. I don't know. What's there to see around here?

DENVER: What's there to see? You have any idea where you are? This is Denver, Colorado, baby-doll – what ISN'T there to see? We could cruise Colfax… go to Tom's Diner… go to Denver Diner… go to the Esquire… China Star… Sancho's… we could go to the Merc.

TUCSON: What's the Merc?

DENVER: Mercury Café.

TUCSON: Hmm… coffee shops and driving around. Sounds like a vacation to me.

DENVER: Come on, it'll be the best kind of vacation. What more does a girl need than watered-down, sugared-up coffee and a genuinely intellectual scene?

TUCSON: I guess you're right. But can you smoke at any of them?

DENVER: No, use to. Not since the ban, can't smoke anywhere anymore. I keep waiting to wake up one morning and find a ticket for smoking in my room.

TUCSON: It's the same way in Tucson.

DENVER: It's the same way everywhere. We could go to Paris on The Platte – you can smoke in there, but the service sucks and it's like you've gotta have an impressive thrift store wardrobe to fit in around there.

TUCSON: Why?

DENVER: Ah, hipsters. Goddamn hipsters are taking this whole town over. This used to be a safe, quiet place to live… that is until the hipsters. *Pause.*

TUCSON: I'm glad I came out here. I know we talked about what we talked about and I'm fine with it... I am. Despite it all, though, I'm still glad I came.

DENVER: Me, too. Now listen, here's the plan for the morning. I have to work at seven. You think you'll be able to keep yourself entertained until I get back?

TUCSON: I'll manage. How are you liking the new job?

DENVER: It's a job. You've washed dishes at one place, you've washed dishes at every place. Lotta yuppies, though. They call this part of town the Highlands and they oughta just call it the Yuppies. My boss and I have been going through this awkward exchange of words since I started. She's got nothing to say to me, I've got nothing to say to her, but yet we try. It's very awkward.

TUCSON: Have you heard anything more from the Jamaicans?

DENVER: Honey, they weren't Jamaicans. They just run a Jamaican style restaurant. And yes, I've heard plenty. The guy keeps sending me text messages. He's taken this whole thing very personally.

TUCSON: Maybe he really liked you.

DENVER: I don't think that's it. I've never had a boss more than moderately tolerate me. I just think he doesn't like to see people leave his restaurant unless he fires them or they're customers. I really wasn't that good. I kept mixing all the lunch plates up with the dinner plates. There was very little difference, but somehow they could see it.

TUCSON: So long as you're happy where you are.

DENVER: I'm happy where I am right now.

TUCSON: Good... me, too. Goodnight, Denver.

DENVER: Goodnight, Tucson.

Lights fade - End of scene.

SCENE 3
SATURDAY NIGHT *shortly before midnight. More sex with music. Red spotlight on the bed serves as only lighting. The Dwarves' song "Saturday Night" plays in background. This scene is played for more of a comedic effect. Lights fade – End of scene.*

SCENE 4
SUNDAY MORNING, *still dark outside, still in bed.*

TUCSON, *slightly self-conscious:* Was it good?

DENVER: Honey, you're fabulous.

TUCSON: I always feel self-conscious about giving bjs. I know I'm doing it right, but it requires so much coordination, and you've gotta use both hands - I have trouble even using one.

DENVER: Yeah, using hands is good.

TUCSON: I'm telling you, there's too much going on. It's hard. Besides, I've already paid my dues.

DENVER: Dues?

TUCSON: Yeah, dues. I used to do it exactly the way Cosmo suggested, but then I realized it didn't really matter, that nobody ever refused one regardless, or complained. Why do all that work if you don't have to?

DENVER: So it was great. You're great. Everything is great. What time is it?

TUCSON: I don't know, let me check... 2:30, a little after.

DENVER: Balls. I gotta be up in four hours.

TUCSON: I'm going to get some water. Want some?

DENVER: Can't I just drink some of yours? I don't want to be responsible for a whole glass. I don't want that much.

She leaves the room. As soon as she does, he pulls his pipe out and starts smoking a bowl and blowing it out the window. She calls to him from the other room. He chokes on the smoke and quickly hides the pipe.

TUCSON: Are you all right?

DENVER: I'm fine.

TUCSON: Why are you coughing?

DENVER: Too many years stuck in the coal mine.

TUCSON: What?

DENVER: Just... damn, may I have some water, please.

She returns to the room with a glass of water. She sits next to him on the bed as he downs the glass of water until it's empty.

TUCSON, *annoyed:* Was it good?

DENVER: Honey, you're fabulous.

SCENE 5
SUNDAY AFTERNOON

She walks in. He's sleeping.

DENVER, *slowly waking up:* Oh. How was your day?

TUCSON: Good. I toured myself around Denver.

DENVER: How did you get around? You took the bus?

TUCSON: Yup.

DENVER: You did?

TUCSON: Yup. I'm very smart. How was work?

DENVER: A lot of dishes are clean today... a lot of dishes are clean today because of me.

TUCSON: Feel pretty good about that, do ya?

DENVER: You have no idea. How was your AA meeting?

TUCSON: It was weird.

DENVER: Why?

TUCSON: They don't do it like they do it in Tucson. It wasn't, um, this isn't the right word, what's the word? Orderly. You know how you're supposed to like wait your turn and you're not supposed to talk while the other people are talking? Well, this one woman kept cutting in and saying, "Oh, uh-huh" and "Yeah, right, that happened to me, too." I'm like, "Lady, what the hell with the crosstalk?" But I wouldn't say it like I'm saying it now. I had an idea for a diplomatic way to tell her to shut the hell up but by the time it was my turn, she finally stopped. *Pause.*

DENVER: So you had a good time?

TUCSON: Yup. So what are you going to do this whole time I'm here... sleep?

DENVER: Portions of it.

TUCSON: Come on, get up.

DENVER: Sweetheart, it's been a very long day. It was a late night, then an early morning, which slowly progressed itself into a long day.

TUCSON: It's three-thirty. Still plenty of day left.

DENVER: Which I will be more than glad to get to after just a few more... several hours of holding perfectly still... with my eyes closed.

TUCSON: So what am I supposed to do?

DENVER: Seize the day? I don't know. What do you feel like doing?

Hinting at sex.

DENVER: Damn, woman. I'm not a machine. I'm a man. A man that requires a reasonable fifteen hours of sleep a day... otherwise I'm no good for anything... or anyone.

She sits back and sighs.

DENVER: Listen, I'm sorry. I am. I'm just beat. Gimmie just a little longer to sleep – no more than an hour and then I'm all yours. I promise. I thought tonight maybe we'd go to the Mercury Café. They're doing the open-mic tonight – you said you wanted to see that, right?

TUCSON: Yeah.

DENVER: Well, all right then... it's a date. We'll take in a little poetry, get some coffee in us, then we can come back here and fuck each other blind.

TUCSON: You're such a romantic.

DENVER: I know, right? I'm not even trying half the time... just comes out of me. Seriously, though... you're good with that? Good with the plan?

TUCSON: Yeah, that sounds fine.

DENVER: Cheers! Back to sleep now. Here we go... back to sleep... starting now.

He lays back down. She sits on the bed and sighs. Then after a moment, she sighs again but louder. After a moment, she sighs once more and once again louder. Finally Denver sits back up.

DENVER: Okay... all right... this isn't... something's not right here.

TUCSON: What do you mean?

DENVER: What do I mean? What do you mean, what do I mean? What's with the sighs, are you outta breath?

TUCSON: No.

DENVER: Because if you're having respiratory problems, I think that's something we need to address.

TUCSON: I'm not having respiratory problems... I'm just having problems – with us.

DENVER: Oh. Well, that's not quite as pressing as respiratory problems... we can probably hold off on addressing that.

TUCSON: You're not funny.

DENVER: Are you sure? I'm trying really hard.

TUCSON: Just forget it.

DENVER: What's wrong?

TUCSON: I don't want to talk about it.

DENVER: Talk about what?

TUCSON: What I don't want to talk about.

Pause.

DENVER: What are you talking about?

TUCSON: I'm not telling you because I know I'm not going to get the answers I want. What's the point? We've already talked about this and you're just going to get all exasperated again and I'm going to be all unsatisfied.

DENVER: Fair enough. Thank you for being considerate of my feelings.

TUCSON: We've been over it all before.

DENVER: Right.

TUCSON: There's nothing more to say about it. I get it. I'm not trying to talk about "our relationship."

DENVER: But by not trying to talk about it... you're sort of talking about it.

TUCSON: Can you just... could you just give me a break here? You've got to understand how stressful it is for me to be here. I mean, it was my choice, but it's hard. I get it, but this conversation is pointless because I already know what you're going to say and you never tell me the things I want to hear anyway and it's just not enough. You're never going to give me enough of what I need.

DENVER: If you already know what I'm going to say, we don't need to talk about it anyway.

TUCSON: I know.

DENVER: You decided you wanted to come out here. And don't get me wrong – I'm glad you're here. But you broke up with me. Because I wasn't giving you enough of what you need, and then you still decided to come out here. So now I'm never going to give you enough – well, that sort of goes both ways, you know what I mean?

TUCSON: I'm not giving you enough?

DENVER: No, you're not giving me enough... slack. I've only been back from California for a few weeks... I'm having to scramble to get things in order and you need to understand how stressful that is for me.

TUCSON: I do.

DENVER: You say that. It's just too much to juggle right now. Trying to put my life in order out here all the while trying to sustain some sort of a relationship over the telephone... and it might not be that taxing if we weren't having to talk everything out every other day. One day things are fine, the next day you're calling me up with some damn laundry list of problems and concerns that you're having and I need to be the one to fix them ultimately by changing something about myself or my routine or I don't even know what anymore.

TUCSON: Let's just drop it. Forget I brought it up.

DENVER: I can do that.

He turns over to go back to sleep.

TUCSON, *noticing the letter on the floor:* You got my letter?

DENVER: Oh, right. I was waiting for you to read it to me.

TUCSON: I'm not reading it to you. I sort of sent it to myself anyway.

DENVER: Sent it to yourself? Well, then it sounds like you're the one that didn't open it. Sure I can't get you to read it?

TUCSON: No, I wrote it a while ago, but I'd already put the stamp on it, and I didn't want to waste the stamp. I planned it so it'd get here while I was visiting.

She opens it, reads it to herself, frowns, and then hides it.

DENVER: Come on, just read it. What do you think I'm going to do? Make fun of you? I wanna hear it.

TUCSON: Fine. If you sing me that song you wrote me, you can read it.

DENVER: No, no, no, never mind. Forget it. I changed my mind.

TUCSON: Come on, you're seriously not going to sing me that song? I came all the way to Denver to hear it.

DENVER: Look, I'm just very insecure about the whole thing. I don't sing well. Just give me a little time to warm up to the idea, all right? Before you leave I'll sing it for you, deal?

TUCSON: Promise? When?

DENVER: When the time is right… the planets align… that sort of thing.

TUCSON: All right. But I'm still not going to read you the letter. You can read it yourself after the song.
DENVER, s*ighs:* Fine.

Denver grabs his guitar and begins to play "The Tucson Song" while he sings off-key.

*The Tucson Song lyrics. (Guitar chords A, D, E, D repeated to a
similar melody as La Bamba.)*

*Well, I got your letter
Glad you're better out in Tucson, Arizona*

*I'm feelin' fine, just passin' time
I guess that some things never change*

*I got an apartment
with an assortment of things that I don't need*

*But I'm glad you asked
I think about the past
Sometimes I just can't help myself*

*A long distance romance
is a kick in the pants
and so is the Goddamn phone bill*

*CHORUS:
The trouble is I'm still in love,
I'm wonderin' if you feel the same.
If nothing else won't you tell me what it is that you do to ease the pain.
It's like the sun always lookin' for the moon,
I'm almost there, but you leave too soon.
So tell me if you care
we'd be quite a pair
I'd comb your hair
with my big teeth.*

*I'd cook your meals
throw away your orange peels
and scrub your heels
and brush your teeth.*

Get the same tattoo
or the same hairdo
get drunk at the zoo
or maybe pierce our teeth.

Cuddle up with our toes
clean each other's nose
with a fire hose
and whistle thru our teeth.

DENVER: Your turn.

TUCSON, *reading:* Up until now, I never really thought you were out there. I'd hoped, without really expecting much, suspecting I'd seen too many romantic comedies and thinking the idea of soul mates was totally ridiculous. Maybe you still think there isn't just one right person out there for you, but I'm really sure right now there is only exactly one perfect fit, like the pair of jeans you wear day after day until they are totally worn out and then spend year upon year upon year wishing you could find them again, only you can't because those were your mom's from the seventies.

DENVER: You stole that.

TUCSON: What? Stole what?

DENVER: That line about the jeans. I said that.

TUCSON: What are you talking about?

DENVER: I told you my mother gave me a pair of her old jeans and they were the best pair of jeans I had ever owned. Then one day they finally couldn't be worn anymore and I still have yet to find a better pair.

TUCSON: You never said that. Those were my mom's jeans I was talking about.

DENVER: Whatever. I'm going back to sleep.

She sits on top of him and starts kissing him. Although it can't be seen, it should be made clear that she has her hand down his pants.

TUCSON: Are you sure you want to sleep some more?

DENVER: That's a clever move, asking me that after you already...

TUCSON, *imitating him:* I know, right? I'm not even trying half the time… just comes out of me.

Lights fade, end of scene.

SCENE 6
LATER SUNDAY AFTERNOON

They're in bed having sex again. Blue Spotlight over bed this time serves as only lighting. "Sunday Kind Of Love" plays in background. This scene is played for more of a romantic effect.

SCENE 7
LATER SUNDAY

They're in bed smoking moments after having sex.

DENVER: Hey, jizz doesn't by any chance taste like coffee, does it?

TUCSON: Just like it.

DENVER: I don't have to do it, especially if you're going to make that look – I felt bad.

TUCSON: What look?

Makes face.

TUCSON: I didn't look like that.

DENVER: That was dead on.

TUCSON: What ever. Come on, let's get out of bed.

DENVER: I feel like... I need like a... like a cheeseburger or something. Could you eat a cheeseburger?

TUCSON: Okay, but let's take a shower first.

DENVER: Uhhhh... I guess I need to take a shower.

TUCSON, *scoffs:* Fine, take your own shower. See ya.

As soon as she leaves, he goes to his closet for his pipe and begins smoking pot out the window. Lights fade – End of scene.

SCENE 8
SUNDAY AFTERNOON

They're both seated on the floor with their backs against the foot of the bed and they're eating cheeseburgers. She has one leg extended over his lap and he's painting her toenails.

DENVER: Don't you feel better? I feel much better.

TUCSON: I smell weed.

DENVER: Probably my roommates. They're very irresponsible people. How's your burger?

TUCSON: Good. How's yours?

DENVER: Delicious!

TUCSON: I'm glad for you. So what time is this thing tonight?

DENVER: Six-thirty... roughly. That's a little early, but it's kinda cool just to hang out down there before things get started.

TUCSON: Are you going to read anything?

DENVER: I was thinking about it. You?

TUCSON: If you do, I will.

DENVER: All right then. Thinking about busting out some old material. I got some impressions I wanna try out.

TUCSON: Impressions?

DENVER: Yeah.

TUCSON: How is that poetry?

DENVER: Not everything in the open-mic has to be poetry. In fact, most of the time, the poetry isn't even poetry. You just get up there and do whatever you want.

TUCSON: Is it far from here?

DENVER: No, it's not too bad. I walked it once. I wouldn't recommend that, but just so you know... I did it.

TUCSON: There's not much... don't get ketchup on my foot...

DENVER: Sorry.

TUCSON: There's not much going on around here, is there?

DENVER: Tell me about it. This part of town sucks. Everybody dresses their dogs up like babies or jogs with their laptops – I've been having a hard time fitting in.

TUCSON: You could jog with your laptop.

DENVER: Yeah, but I don't have a laptop and, uh, oh yeah, I don't jog – so, no… I couldn't. It's just like nothing ever happens here. Sometimes I have to fight this urge to throw myself into traffic just to make something interesting happen. Or maybe not myself, but maybe like kick one of those little baby dogs into traffic, just to mix things up a little.

TUCSON: I know what you mean. My cousin used to say that whenever she walked across a bridge – and not because she was suicidal because she wasn't – but she'd say that she was afraid she would get the urge just to jump off. Like she would just lose control over her impulses.

DENVER: Yeah, well, my first year in college my buddies and me went camping in the mesas and we were set up like 30 or 40 feet – I don't know, I'm not good with measurements – point is, we're real close to this ledge, just this enormous drop into the canyons and we're all sitting near the edge just looking at it. And this was back before I drank, smoked, anything like that, but I suddenly felt this urge to jump off. And it wasn't like I was depressed or wanting to die or anything. I was happy. I was in school, had my health, my student loans weren't due, I didn't have any credit cards, life was good. But yet I wanted to jump. I told my buddies and it turned out they were thinking the same thing. So it must be a common feeling.

TUCSON: I've had it before, too, but in a different way... like when I see happy families with babies… like I might just take one.

DENVER: Yeah, I wouldn't repeat that to too many people. Let me have your other foot.

TUCSON: You're pretty good at that.

DENVER: Are you done with your burger?

TUCSON: Yeah, I gave it my best.

DENVER: May I have it, please?

TUCSON: If I can have one of your cigarettes.

DENVER: Deal.

He gives her a cigarette as she hands him the burger. Lights fade – End of scene.

SCENE 9
SUNDAY NIGHT

They return home to the bedroom. Denver is depressed and makes a bee line straight for the bed. He throws himself down face first and begins to scream in rage into the blankets. Tucson stands in the background, taking off her jacket and observing him. Once he stops screaming, he calmly looks up from the blankets and speaks to her.

DENVER: Listen, I don't want you to get the wrong idea about tonight.

TUCSON: What do you mean?

DENVER: I mean, I bombed... and that's... just not how I typically roll.

TUCSON: You were fine.

DENVER: Yes, I was fine.

TUCSON: And that's the problem?

DENVER: Yes! That's the sucker of cock problem. I'm not fine. I'm great! Like that cartoon tiger for that... whatever that cereal's called.

TUCSON: Well, yeah, but that tiger, he's worked at it for years and you...

DENVER: Sure, take his side. Wouldn't be the first time.

TUCSON: You're being ridiculous. So you usually do better. So what?

DENVER: You wouldn't understand.

TUCSON: What's that supposed to mean?

DENVER: I don't know. I just sorta said it, I'm sorry. Listen, I just... I'm not that good at like a lot of things, ya know? I got like two things at best that I'm really good at. I can parallel park like nobody's business and then I can write. That's who I am. Anybody can tell you. Pull any guy off the street and ask him about me... provided he knew who I was and we had like spent a significant portion of our childhood together... and he'll tell you I parallel park like a mother fucker and I write just the same. But I don't know... it's like I lost it.

TUCSON: Well... maybe you shouldn't have sold your car.

DENVER: All right, Paula Poundstone. Since when did you turn into such a comedian?

TUCSON: I don't know. Tonight I guess. I got that really good laugh after that line about my tits being deflated and I just feel... great.

DENVER: You're killing me, do you realize that? With every word you speak, a little more of me dies.

TUCSON: I think you're over-reacting. So they didn't laugh that much. You're out of practice, you said so yourself. How long has it been since you were back there?

DENVER: Too long.

TUCSON: So there you go. And, hey, that guy we met dedicated his poem to us – "To The Story of Us." That was great – and I haven't heard you say one thing about that.

DENVER: Ah, he was drunk.

TUCSON: Whatever. You're too negative. You're too hard on yourself and you're too negative. You talk about being blocked, well, that's probably why. You're trying too hard. If you could just relax…

DENVER: Yeah, well, that's a lot easier said than done. Relax – what does that even mean?

TUCSON: In the long run, I don't know. But for the time that I'm here, ya know, it would be nice if you could be a little more… present.

DENVER: We've talked about this. My present mood will always be determined by the present state of my work. I can't control that – it's who I am. I'm sorry I haven't been much fun since you've been out here. I knew this was just bad timing.

TUCSON: Are you even happy I'm here?

DENVER: Of course I am. But you won't always be.

TUCSON: Sometimes I wish you'd never come back to Denver. When you were still in California you had all the time and energy in the world to talk on the phone with me. Two and three hours every night. And you got pissed off when you thought it was my turn to call and you were waiting by the phone.

DENVER: That worked then, but it's different now. Talking on the phone is not a relationship. It's a phone call. You ever see two people get married over the phone? Have sex, raise kids, over the phone? It's not enough. And I know we've talked about you moving out here, but... I just don't know that I'm ready. If somehow you could move here and have your own place, your own friends, your own things to do... that would be one thing. But moving in together right away? And you said yourself, you don't want to live with someone unless you're married... well, I'm not ready to get married. I still like smoking weed. I still like getting drunk. I still like staying out all night and having nobody to answer to. That's still who I am.

TUCSON: Well, you're lucky I'm smart enough not to move out here.

DENVER: I do feel bad about you leaving. Especially after tonight. Aside from the performance, yeah, you know, tonight was great. It was great being there with you... like a real couple, ya know. But as soon as I felt that, I immediately shut it out because after Tuesday it'll be gone. And then it's back to the grindstone. Trying to get a play finished, trying to get it produced, trying to get people there, trying to get back in the papers – trying, ya know. And this is all I feel like I have time for. *Pause.*

TUCSON: All right, how about this – we'll make a list. Tell me all the things you're stressed out about.

DENVER: I don't know, I mean I do, but... I've just – I've been blocked. Feels like I got stress from a lot of different directions – other things that demand my attention.

TUCSON: Like what?

DENVER: Working. Making enough to pay bills, rent, that sorta thing. And I hate to be the kind of guy that uses something like that as an excuse to not get any work done – but it's difficult. Draining. Frustrating. Starting a bunch of things, but lacking....

TUCSON: Execution?

DENVER: Yes, exactly, execution – I lack that.

TUCSON: Well, what can we do about it?

DENVER: We? Uh, I don't know that it works that way.

TUCSON: What way?

DENVER: Joint effort. To me writing has always been like taking a shit.

TUCSON: What?

DENVER: Just listen. You're all plugged up, right? Can't get anything out – and it's painful. It's ever so painful. But then that special moment finally comes and you need privacy to like... get it all out. And it feels ever so good. *Pause.* And you can't very well have someone kneeling beside you, holding your hand, coaching you through it.

TUCSON: No, I get it. But I think it's different. Taking a shit is so easy, so common. I feel like it's worse than that. It's like the waiting for an orgasm when you're trying too hard to have one because all you want is the end so you can get some fucking sleep and your mind can fucking quit running circles around everything that's happening and not happening and what you're doing with your life or not doing and finally, fucking finally take a vacation from all that shit. *Pause.*

DENVER: No, I like mine better.

TUCSON: Have you ever tried working with someone else?

DENVER: No. No, I don't believe I have.

TUCSON: So how do you know it wouldn't work?

DENVER: Well, I… it just doesn't… well, what'd you have in mind?

TUCSON: Us. We write the story of us.

DENVER: Ah, come on.

TUCSON: I'm serious.

DENVER: So am I. Who's going to pay money to come see a play about the two of us?

TUCSON: Maybe they won't. Maybe it'll never see the light of day. But it'd be good practice… ease back into things… and maybe land on some sort of closure for us in the process.

DENVER: So, what are you saying – we just write about how we met?

TUCSON: No. We write this trip. These four days together. I'll write a line and then you write a line and we'll go back and forth until it's finished.

DENVER: I don't know.

TUCSON: Come on. It'll be fun.

DENVER: Do you even remember everything we've said?

TUCSON: You have no idea.

Lights fade – End of scene

SCENE 10
MONDAY

In the bedroom with paper spread about the place. They're writing the play.

TUCSON: Hey.

DENVER: What?

TUCSON: I never said this.

DENVER: Said what?

TUCSON: I never said coffee tasted like jizz.

DENVER: You most certainly did. I sat right here and listened to you say it.

TUCSON: Well, I didn't mean it.

DENVER: Well, who's to say you mean it in the play? It's just funny. People'll laugh at it… hopefully.

TUCSON: This is turning into… well, it's very personal.

DENVER: Personal?

TUCSON: Yeah, like you have in here that we're doing it like every two seconds.

DENVER: Hey, sweetness, keep in mind this was your idea. And it's working.

TUCSON, *sighs:* Let's have sex.

DENVER: Right now?

TUCSON: We've been writing all morning. Let's just take a break.

DENVER: All right, let me just finish this up.

He proceeds to write as she begins to undress herself. Once she's mostly undressed, he looks up and notices her standing there with a seductive pose.

DENVER: Okay, I'm ready.

TUCSON: Thought so.

They both climb into bed, under the covers and assume their positions. A moment goes by and then she realizes that he's still writing.

TUCSON: What are you doing?

DENVER: What's it look like I'm doing? I'm rockin' your world!

TUCSON: Shut up, I see what you're doing. Are you writing about this right now?

DENVER: What? What are you talking about? Of course not.

TUCSON: You are. I know you are. Whatever. Just tell me what you're writing.

DENVER: I'm writing the truth! Just stop talking, you're fuckin' up my concentration.

TUCSON: Give it to me!

DENVER: I'm trying to! Hold still.

TUCSON: No, give me the paper, jackass. *She takes it from him.*

TUCSON, *reading what he has written:* "He sexed her good… and she was never the same…" This is retarded.

DENVER: It's my art!

TUCSON: If you're going to do this, then we're doing it the right way.

Still having sex, she grabs the pen and begins writing. She continues to write the entire time they have sex.

TUCSON: Start from the beginning… what did you first say?
DENVER: When?

TUCSON: Something about concentration.

DENVER: Yes! You're fucking up my concentration. Write that down.

TUCSON: Oh, that feels good. Okay, what'd I say?

DENVER: I don't remember… I was concentrating.

TUCSON: Oh, oh, oh! Give it to me!

DENVER: I'm fuckin' trying!

TUCSON: No, that's what I said.

DENVER: Oh… right… sorry.

TUCSON: And then I said… and then I said…

DENVER: Yeah, yeah, tell me what you said…

TUCSON: I said… give me the paper… jackass!

DENVER: This is my art! This is my art!

TUCSON: Oh, give it to me! Give me your art!

DENVER: Are you still writing?

TUCSON: I'm writing, I'm writing!

DENVER: Keep writing, keep writing, oh, sweet Christ, don't stop!

TUCSON: Oh! I never said... coffee tastes... like jizz!

DENVER: You most certainly did! I sat... right here... and listened to you!

TUCSON: This is very personal, oh!

DENVER: People will laugh, oh God! They'll laugh!

TUCSON: Have sex with me...

DENVER: I'm ready...

TUCSON: Have sex with me...

DENVER: I'm ready! I'm ready!

TUCSON: Me, too! Don't stop!

And by a small act of God they both manage to climax simultaneously but played for a comedic effect. Pause as she climbs off of him and they both lie in bed, winded. He lights two cigarettes.

DENVER: Did you get all that?

Lights fade – End of scene

SCENE 11
MONDAY NIGHT

TUCSON, *in bed writing:* I think that your character should be more sensitive and less arrogant. He wants everybody to think he's a playa without any real deep feelings, just a guy in a tough spot because he's got all these different things pulling at him. But he's a better guy than that. At least, I hope so.

DENVER: I hope so, too.

TUCSON: I'm serious, you're not this obnoxious in real life...are you?

DENVER: I don't see my character as being obnoxious – quite frankly I'm offended... my character is offended. Look, we're so close to having it done – let's just finish it first and then we can fine tune things, all right?

TUCSON: And what about this? The Cosmo. You make it sound like I don't make a single decision in life without consulting Cosmo.

DENVER: I only put it in there because it's come up in conversation more than once.

TUCSON: I have to change this part. It would never say that the number one reason men don't perform well in the bedroom has to do with their heart not being in it.

DENVER: Does it really make you feel weird that this play is all about sex? I mean, it's as if we're just two people who can't get out of bed and do anything. Don't get me wrong – the sex is great, but it's not all we are, all we do. I mean, what about these characters' identities? What is there to make people care?

TUCSON: A lot. This stuff really happened, for one thing. These characters are authentic. Nobody needs or wants to know what our day jobs are or any of the other minuscule details that don't have anything to do with our four days. We're just Denver and Tucson... not Daria and Irvine, or anybody else more specific. I like it that way.

DENVER: Yeah, but it's lacking something. Right now it just feels like it's a non-specific male voice talking to a non-specific female voice and there's nothing that makes them real. They're lacking some sort of identity.

TUCSON: What do people want to know? That I spend all my food stamps on four dollar protein shakes? That I file my bank statements? That I feel sorry for George Bush? What do people wanna know? How do I give something to care about?

DENVER: Can I write that?

TUCSON: What matters is that she's struggling to figure out how she's going to get what she needs, or else accept that she's never gonna get it.

DENVER, *not paying attention to the significance of what she has just said:* Yeah, yeah, yeah, that's good. That's what I'm talking about – it needs more of that. Help me write that down.

TUCSON, *almost says more to herself:* Sometimes I think this play makes it seem like I don't care about myself all that much. That I'm weak for coming to Denver. That I'm fucked up for spending four days in bed with this guy. That I should have left.

DENVER, *not paying attention:* You know, I don't think this is half bad. I'll admit, I had my doubts, but, shit… this is kind of funny.

TUCSON, *she stands at the edge of the stage and delivers this speech to the audience:* Our play is R-rated. It's making me uncomfortable. This play shouldn't just be about making people squirm in their seats with vicarious pleasure, although they should. It's more than that. I don't want people judging my character. I want people to know that she has her reasons for doing the things she does. It'd be easy to say they both act out from growing up in dysfunctional families or are just masochistic, insecure, or have addictive personalities. I think they truly love each other. Maybe they're just both scared half to death that the other person doesn't feel the same way, and they don't have a better way to act it out than in bed. Because it's just four days, and after that, what? It'll be back to five minute phone calls.

DENVER: You know, I'll bet I could make a few phone calls to some people and get this produced. I mean, not overnight or anything… but I'll bet I could get this done.

TUCSON: The night we met we were full of ourselves, and whatever characters we were playing smacked right into each other. The romance was that nobody knew what would happen in the next five minutes, let alone the next year, or forever. Who cared? When somebody asks me to marry them, I'll always say sure. Not that I actually intend to, but it'd make a good story to tell our kids. When I found out, which I should have assumed then, that was his line, I laughed. I know that the exact guy I'll marry someday will use a line like that, which made it even better.

DENVER: What about a title? Jesus, we haven't even talked about a title. We could call it something like "4 Day Sex Romp"… leave your kids at home – something catchy like that, I don't know, we can work on it later.

TUCSON: I had mixed feelings about visiting Denver. I owed it to him, I think. Besides, I never want to be the kind of girl who doesn't go to Denver. But now he's got these other concerns and priorities, and he can't back up any of the promises he's made with actions because he's more worried about his career, his future, his wild oats or whatever the hell they are. And no matter how many times he's said that's all it is, that he's fucking stressed out about his life, she doesn't believe him, that he loves her. What's she gonna do, anyway? Wait around until he grows up? Who knows how long that's gonna take, or if there'll even be any payoff? If there'll even be a next act? She deserves better anyhow, and more. They haven't even said "I love you." Maybe they won't. Maybe that line doesn't even make it into the play.

DENVER: Hey, what do you think about if my character wears glasses? I mean, I know I don't actually wear glasses but I always wished I did. Maybe this'll be my one and only chance – what do you think?

TUCSON: Yeah, fine.

DENVER: Yeah?

TUCSON: That sounds great. I'm going to the bathroom.

She leaves the room. He waits for a minute and then grabs his pipe and a fake pair of glasses. As he smokes, he addresses the audience.

DENVER: All right, listen… I know it may seem like I'm, uh, insensitive or some damn thing… but I'm not. You don't know the whole story. This is our second stab at this. This is how it goes… about a year ago around this time I'm out in Tucson doing a show at this coffee house… I can't ever remember the name of the place… Goddammit, if she was still in here she could tell you. Anyway, I'm doing this show and she's in the audience. The show finishes and we go out for ice cream because she says she doesn't drink. We sat on this curb for hours eating ice cream and telling each other our "secrets" because she figures we're never going to see each other again. She tells me something about a fortune cookie she got and it said something about her getting married in the next year. So I made a light joke about coming back to Tucson and getting married… and then she said okay. Still with me? All right, so we kiss and then I go back home to Denver. A week later, I've scraped as much cash I could together and I'm on a Greyhound back to Tucson to see her – a woman who I've really only known in person for less than five hours. Sure, we had phone calls in between that time, but what's a phone call, right? I've been saying that all along. So I get out there and it's great – I'm talking about moving out there, talking about marriage, and it seems like the beginning of the rest of our lives. But then on the third day she gets cold feet. Starts telling me things are moving too fast, which they were… but that was kind of the idea. She tells me she's got some unfinished business with some other guy who comes around from time to time and she'd like to slow things down and continue seeing both of us casually. And I tell her normally that would be reasonable, that is if I already lived in Tucson. But I'm not going to move to another state just so I can share her with some asshole I don't even know... even if I did know him, fuck him, you know what I mean? So I leave. Head back to Denver, broke in the pockets and broke in the heart. My bus leaves me in Los Cruces, New Mexico and as I'm stranded in this town for nine or so hours I make a decision – this is the last time. I've made more bonehead decisions over women and then paid for them dearly and I'm burned out. I haven't spent my whole life dreaming of being someone's husband. It's relatively easy to fall in love. To find someone, tell 'em you love 'em, get married, buy a house and spend the rest of your lives driving each other crazy – that's easy. But following your dream... seeing it through to the end? Therein lies the challenge. I just spent five months getting my ass handed to me out in LA and now I'm back here having to answer to all of these people and all of their questions... "How was Hollywood? Did you make it big? How was your show? Are you famous yet? How come you're back here if you're famous?" Point is, I believe love finds you when the time is right. Until that time... be as selfish as you possibly can be – or spend the rest of your life regretting it. I didn't always think this way, but that doesn't matter – I do now. *She comes back into the bedroom and he climbs into bed.* Hey, what was the name of that coffee shop we met at?

TUCSON: Bentley's.

He gives the audience a look.

TUCSON: I'm sooooo tired.

DENVER: Are you too tired to...

TUCSON: I'm not that tired.

DENVER: Awesome. I'll get the paper.

TUCSON: Wait. I think... maybe just for one time... we don't write about it.

DENVER: Really?

TUCSON: Just once, I'd like it to be private... just for us.

DENVER: All right. I hear you.

She climbs into bed with him. They kiss as lights fade – End of Scene

SCENE 12
MONDAY NIGHT

They're in bed smoking – shortly after sex.

TUCSON: How do you think we should end it?

DENVER: End what?

TUCSON: The play.

DENVER: I don't know. Maybe we'll just let it play out.

TUCSON: But what if that's not exciting enough?

DENVER: What? You think we should make something up?

TUCSON: Maybe.

DENVER: Like what?

TUCSON: Just start throwing things out there... we'll try it all until something sticks.

DENVER: All right. Uh, zombie invasion.

TUCSON: What?

DENVER: Yeah, the classic zombie invasion. Like we've been held up in this bedroom for days… no food… no water…

TUCSON: Just cigarettes and coffee?

DENVER: Exactly. A zombie's worst fear. But it's finally come to a point of escaping or die trying. You with me?

TUCSON: Till the end.

Zombies bust through the back wall and start attacking. Denver and Tucson start shooting at them with their pretend guns. They don't stop until all of them are dead.

TUCSON: I don't know if I like that ending.

DENVER: Too graphic?

TUCSON: It has nothing to do with us.

DENVER: I know, but it's all about entertainment. Gotta give the people what they want. What about a Cops ending?

TUCSON: What's a Cops ending?

DENVER: You've never seen the show, Cops?

TUCSON: Of course I've seen it. So what?

DENVER: So act accordingly.

Two police officers enter through the hole in the wall and begin to handcuff Denver. They begin to act out classic redneck arrest.

TUCSON: Don't you take him! Don't you take him! He's a good man! He hits cuz he loves!

DENVER: You tell 'em, mama! You fuckin' pigs! If it's a crime to live in this country, smoke a bunch of PCP and run yer old lady over with the car, then I hereby tender my resignation to the United States for which it stands! *He spits.*

TUCSON: What am I gonna tell the babies? What do I tell my babies!

DENVER: Tell 'em fight for their right to party! That's what you tell 'em. Whisper it into their majestic ears while they sleep.

TUCSON: I love you.

DENVER: I love you. *Being dragged away.* Don't let the kids drink all my beer! And don't get fat! *They exit through the hole in the wall. After a moment, Denver returns.*

DENVER: No good?

TUCSON: Closer, but not quite.

DENVER: Well, you come up with something then.

TUCSON: What about like a Shakespearean ending?

DENVER: Love and loss?

TUCSON: Everybody dies.

DENVER: I'm into it, let's do it. *They get into position.*

TUCSON: Oh... oh, Denver... I've poisoned myself.

DENVER: Word?

TUCSON: I thought you were gone forever.

DENVER: No. Alas... I was simply out of town.

TUCSON: A phone call t'would have done my feeble soul good.

DENVER: Oh, dearest Tucson... I had no bars where my feet stood.

TUCSON: Oh... 'tis no matter now. For now we both shall die and live on together as one for eternity.

DENVER: Uh... I'm not... I'm not actually poisoned.

TUCSON: There's a little bit left in the bottle... a drop or two... just enough to take you with me.

DENVER: Right, well, now... uh, let's just think about this.

TUCSON: Think about what, my sweet prince? Don't you love me?

DENVER: For shizzle. But like, uh, I don't know that killing myself is the best way to show that.

TUCSON: What ever do you mean?

DENVER: For instance, I could send your parents a very lovely flower arrangement. Something that said I loved your daughter... but it's cool, I'll move on.

TUCSON: My parents both tragically took their own lives in the second act!

DENVER: Oh, that's right... you got like godparents or something?

TUCSON: Please, darling... I feel myself fading more and more by the moment. The poison... take it to your lips.

DENVER: I just don't know how comfortable...

TUCSON: Hurry! Before it's too late.

DENVER: Fine! Fuck! To be honest, this is why we weren't working out so well beforehand. It's always gotta be your shit... what you want... what you need...

TUCSON: I can't feel my legs.

DENVER: Yeah, well, that's poison for you. How about you try some other options before jumping right to suicide next time, huh? *Drinking the poison.* A guy can't leave town for a couple of days... get his head straight... too much to ask. *They both die.*

DENVER: I don't know. Seems like a bad idea to end on such a downer.

TUCSON: Maybe you're right. Let's try doing it more realistically.

DENVER: What do you mean? *She grabs her bag.*

TUCSON: Okay. We're at the airport... so what's your line?

DENVER: All right. It's been nice seeing you.

TUCSON: Are you glad I came?

DENVER: Of course I am.

TUCSON: How can I be for sure?

DENVER: What do you mean? I just told you.

TUCSON: Tell me in a different way.

DENVER: What do you... like in a different language?

TUCSON: No, not in a different language. In another way than just saying the words. There has to be more to why I came out here – it wasn't just for sex, it wasn't just to write a play – so tell me why I came out here.

DENVER: I don't know what you mean! I never know what you're talking about. You came out here, uh, because you wanted to and, uh, you got time off from work.

TUCSON: I need more than that. I can't spell it out for you – not anymore than I already have.

DENVER: Fuck! Can I have a clue?

TUCSON: You don't need one.

DENVER: I really think that I might. Look, I'm sorry I'm not enough for you. I'm sorry I'm disappointing. I never led you on – everything I've ever said to you I meant. It's just that where I'm at and where you're at aren't the same places – we've got to just, uh, uh, accept that – you know. I'm sorry! I'm so sorry for everything, all right? But it doesn't mean… it never meant that I don't love you. *She smirks.* That's it, isn't it? Damn. I love you. I love you! Jesus Christ Almighty – Tucson, Arizona, I love you!!

TUCSON: Was that so hard?

DENVER: It kind of was. *They kiss.*

TUCSON, *turning to the audience:* The End.

CURTAIN

www.ingramcontent.com/pod-product-compliance
Lightning Source LLC
Chambersburg PA
CBHW021521240626
47154CB00002B/727